W9-BTP-479

RECEIVED

MAY 1 7 2012

By

In the Bag

No Longer the Property of
Hayner Public Library District

HAYNER PUBLIC LIBRARY DISTRICT
ALTON, ILLINOIS

OVERDUES 10 PER DAY, MAXIMUM FINE
COST OF ITEM
ADDITIONAL $5.00 SERVICE CHARGE
APPLIED TO
LOST OR DAMAGED ITEMS

HAYNER PLD/ALTON SQUARE

In the Bag

KATE KLISE

WILLIAM MORROW

An Imprint of HarperCollins*Publishers*

Grateful acknowledgment is made to reprint from "MacArthur Park" and "Wichita Lineman." Words and Music by Jimmy Webb. Copyright © 1968 UNIVERSAL–POLYGRAM INTERNATIONAL PUBLISHING, INC. Copyright Renewed. All Rights Reserved. Used by Permission. *Reprinted by permission of Hal Leonard Corporation.*

This book is a work of fiction. The characters, incidents, and dialogue are drawn from the author's imagination and are not to be construed as real. Any resemblance to actual events or persons, living or dead, is entirely coincidental.

IN THE BAG. Copyright © 2012 by Kate Klise. All rights reserved. Printed in the United States of America. No part of this book may be used or reproduced in any manner whatsoever without written permission except in the case of brief quotations embodied in critical articles and reviews. For information address HarperCollins Publishers, 10 East 53rd Street, New York, NY 10022.

HarperCollins books may be purchased for educational, business, or sales promotional use. For information please write: Special Markets Department, HarperCollins Publishers, 10 East 53rd Street, New York, NY 10022.

FIRST EDITION

Designed by Diahann Sturge

Library of Congress Cataloging-in-Publication Data has been applied for.

ISBN 978-0-06-210805-0

12 13 14 15 16   OV/RRD   10 9 8 7 6 5 4 3 2 1

b19983852

Ladies and gentlemen, as we start our descent, please make sure your seat backs and tray tables are in their locked and upright position. Make sure your seat belt is securely fastened and all carry-on luggage is stowed underneath the seat in front of you or in the overhead bins. Please turn off all electronic devices until we are safely parked at the gate. Thank you.

In the Bag

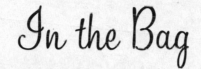

PASSPORT

United States of America

BOARDING PASS

American Airlines

BOARDING PASS
DAISY M. SPRINKLE

FROM:
Chicago - ORD
TO:
Paris - CDG

FLIGHT
42

SEAT
6B

DATE
APR16

DEPARTS
5:55PM

ARRIVES
9:10AM

DATE CLASS
APR16 P

DEPARTS
5:55PM

SEAT
6B

ELECTRONIC

BOARDING PASS

American Airlines

BOARDING PASS
ANDREW NELSON

FROM:
Chicago - ORD
TO:
Paris - CDG

FLIGHT
42

SEAT
13C

DEPARTS
5:55PM

ARRIVES
9:10AM

DATE CLASS
APR16 L

DEPARTS
5:55PM

SEAT
13C

Day 1: Sunday

Dear Ms. 6B,

Please forgive my clumsiness while boarding. I would be more than happy to pay for the cleaning or replacement of your blouse. Truth is, I would be even happier if you'd let me take you to dinner sometime when we return to our side of the pond. That is, if you do plan to return to the U.S. (For all I know, you could be Parisian. You have That Look.)

Charles de Gaulle

CocoChi@com

CHAPTER I

Webb

*O*h, God.

I saw the problem as soon as I unzipped my black duffel bag. There in two neat piles sat clothes that were definitely not mine.

Colorful new T-shirts (size S). Ironed jeans. (*Who irons jeans?*) Flip-flops. High-heeled sandals. A skirt. A gypsy-looking blouse thing. And flowered underwear and bras.

"Oh, God," I said again, this time out loud and with a low groan.

"What's wrong?" Dad asked. He was walking out of the bathroom wearing a hotel robe and drying his hair with a towel.

"This isn't my stuff," I said.

"What do you mean?" Dad replied.

"This bag," I said. "It's not mine. I must've picked up somebody else's bag at the airport."

Dad sighed. "Oh, God, Webb." As always, it sounded like *Oh, cobweb*.

A half hour before this conversation, we'd checked into the Palace Hotel in the heart of Madrid. Dad had been hired to design an exhibit at a nearby contemporary art museum. The show was scheduled to open in two days, which meant Dad would be busy with work and I'd be free to spend my spring break urban hiking. That's why I'd packed my favorite boots.

And now what did I have? High-heeled sandals, a gypsy blouse, and bras.

"What do I do?" I asked, sitting on the bed on my side of the hotel room.

"Call the airline," Dad said. "If your bag's still in Paris, they'll put it on a plane and get it here. We can ask, anyway." He didn't sound encouraging. "Is that your backpack?"

"Yeah," I said, kicking the green nylon bag at my feet.

"And did you have your other bag when we went through Customs in Paris?"

I tried to remember. I'd slept for most of the flight. I was barely awake when we went through the Customs line.

"They didn't open my bags," I recalled, digging through my backpack in search of my cell phone. That's when I remembered.

"Oh, no," I said.

"Now what?"

"I think I left my phone at school."

Dad sighed again, this time louder. "Do you have your baggage claim ticket? Or your boarding passes?"

I rummaged through the pockets of my jeans: gum wrappers, a dime, a dusty Tic Tac. "I don't know."

Dad walked over to the desk chair where he'd thrown his jacket. He emptied the pockets.

"Here," he said, holding up a fistful of papers. "So at least we know what flights we were on. American Airlines flight 854 connecting to flight 42. Then, Air France flight 1600 from Paris to Madrid."

"Uh-huh," I mumbled.

"And of course," Dad continued, "you had a tag on your bag." He paused. "Webb, please tell me you had a tag on your bag with your name on it."

"Yeah," I said tentatively. "I think I did. I mean, I'm pretty sure I did. Wait. Did I?"

"Oh, God, Webb."

Coco

O h, shit!"

"What's wrong?" Mom asked from the bedroom.

She'd been nice enough to offer me the bedroom, but I really did prefer the futon in the living room. All I had to do was open the wooden shutters and I could look out and see Paris. *Paris!*

I'd been waiting for this moment for months. For Christmas, Mom had given me a black duffel bag from L.L.Bean filled with Paris guidebooks. I'd spent much of the flight from Chicago highlighting all the things I wanted to see during my spring break.

Now all I wanted to do was kill myself.

"*Shit!*" I said again.

"You know I hate that word," Mom said, walking the short

distance from the bedroom to the living room of our borrowed apartment on rue des Trois-Frères.

"Well, I hate myself," I answered, flopping on the futon.

"What *is* it?" Mom demanded.

But one look at the grubby wad of clothes in the middle of the floor answered her question. Instead of the clothes I had carefully chosen and meticulously packed, she saw a pile of old T-shirts, dirty jeans (*Who packs unwashed jeans?*), stinky hiking boots, boxer shorts, and one wrinkled white shirt.

"Whose stuff is that?" Mom asked.

"I don't know," I answered.

"Then how'd you get it? And where's your bag?"

"I don't *know*," I said icily. And then I hated myself even more for snapping at my mom. I swallowed hard and tried again. "I somehow picked up the wrong bag at the airport. I'm such an idiot."

"You're not an idiot," Mom insisted. She looked around the room. "Do you have your book bag?"

"Yeah," I said. "I had that with me on the plane. It's the other bag—the bag I checked."

"Okay, did you have *both* bags when we went through Customs?"

I thought back to the line we'd stood in at the airport. I was carrying two bags. The Customs agent had looked at me and then at my passport. Then he stamped it, and that was it.

"Nobody opened my bags," I said. "So I don't know if I had the right one even then." I could feel hot tears burning in my eyes.

"It's okay," Mom said. "We'll go back to the airport and get your bag. It's not a big deal. Just give me five minutes to change clothes. I've got to get out of this blouse. I smell like vinegar."

She turned and promptly stubbed her toe on a table.

"*Shit,*" she said. And she hobbled down the hall to the bedroom.

CHAPTER 3

Andrew

*O*h, hell.

What had I done? Webb thought I was being short-tempered with him about the bag. And granted, that was one complication we didn't need. But the truth was, I was kicking myself for something I'd done earlier in the day.

Here I had one of the biggest commissions of the year—designing an exhibit of digital art at the Palacio de Cristal in Madrid—but instead of working on my final notes for the show, I spent the entire flight from Chicago to Paris obsessing about a woman sitting in first class.

I saw her as we were boarding. She was already seated, reading a magazine and drinking a complimentary glass of red wine from a real glass. (Ah, the privileges of first-class travel.) I was glad to be walking behind Webb so I could linger a bit longer over this vision in seat 6B. I willed her to raise her eyes from the magazine so I could see her face better, but she was engrossed in a recipe. I tried to see what it was. Something *gra-*

tin? Something *rustique*? I was struggling to read upside down.

And that's when Webb stopped to help an elderly passenger load a roller bag in the overhead compartment. I walked right into my son and lost my balance. It was only for a split second, but long enough for me to bump Ms. 6B's arm just as she was raising the glass to her lips.

"Dammit!" I said as she spilled red wine down the front of her blouse. "I'm so sorry."

"Oh!" said the woman, her eyes on the stain.

"Can I—" I started to say.

But a flight attendant swooped in with a damp cloth. "Here, let me blot," she told Ms. 6B. And then like a stern nurse she ordered me to take my seat. "*Now.*"

I spent the next eight hours in a fog of mental distraction and physical contortion.

If I twisted my neck to an absurd angle, I could see her from my aisle seat in row thirteen. I watched her cross her legs, first in one direction and then the other. She was wearing attractive black shoes that she slipped off early into the flight. How old was she? Forty? Maybe forty-five?

I watched as she coiled her golden-brown ponytail around itself until it became a bun. A bun? No, that sounds like something from my mother's generation, and this was definitely a postmodern woman. Witness her rectangular glasses— so chic and architectural. The perfect frame for her angular face. In a previous era, she might've been a noblewoman who modeled for Botticelli.

Best of all, I didn't see anyone sitting next to her. For a moment I almost regretted cashing in my first-class ticket, provided by the client, to buy coach-class tickets for Webb and me. Neither of us fit comfortably in the seats, especially not my six-foot, four-inch son.

But there we were in row thirteen. While Webb watched the god-awful Adam Sandler movie, I drafted the note in my head. When Webb finally closed his eyes to sleep, I pulled a piece of paper from my briefcase and began writing.

Dear MS. 6B,

Please forgive my clumsiness while boarding. I would be more than happy to pay for the cleaning or replacement of your blouse. Truth is, I would be even happier if you'd let me take you to dinner sometime when we return to our side of the pond. That is, if you do plan to return to the U.S. (For all I know, you could be Parisian. You have That Look.)

Were I traveling alone, I might be bolder and introduce myself to you when we land. But for now, all I can do is invite you to e-mail me if you're interested in meeting an admirer who feels terrible about ruining your travel attire.

Most sincerely,
Mr. 13C
My e-mail: lineman@com

P.S. You are truly first class.

I immediately regretted the P.S. It bordered on sleazy, but I liked the way it balanced the note. I hoped she'd read it with a wry smile. She looked like a woman with a sense of irony, the kind of character you see in BBC dramas. A Kate-Winslet-esque actress who wears red lipstick and a silk slip.

I wondered if I'd really have the nerve to give the note to the woman. Probably not. I'd never done anything even remotely like this before. Who *did* this kind of thing? Desperate men. Lonely men. Single fathers with teenage sons.

I decided to do it. Why not? Why the *hell* not? What did I have to lose? *Yes,* I thought. *I'll do it!*

I waited until we'd landed at Charles de Gaulle and were collecting our luggage at the baggage claim area. Webb and I had to catch our connecting flight to Madrid at the Air France terminal, so there was no time to waste.

"Grab your bag and let's go," I told Webb. I'd already spotted Ms. 6B by the baggage carousel.

She was taller than I'd thought. Prettier, too, with an air of self-confidence. Her face looked freshly washed. Her hair was pulled back in the original ponytail. The style nicely set off her long neck. I liked her choice of travel clothes: wide-leg black slacks and a short black jacket that covered her ruined blouse. But mostly I liked her face. The narrow nose. The way her lips formed an involuntary smile. She looked strong but kind, even after a transatlantic flight.

I brushed past her, close enough to see she wore no rings on her left hand. Then I stuck the note in her bag.

I did it! I thought. *I DID IT!* Two seconds later my mind shifted to: *Why did I do that?*

"Come on, Webb," I ordered under my breath. "Get your bag and let's go—*now*."

It was my fault he'd grabbed the wrong bag.

Oh, hell.

CHAPTER 4

Daisy

Oh, please.

I didn't even see it until we were back at the airport, looking for my daughter's bag. Coco was paging through a laminated book, trying to find the picture that best matched her black duffel bag. I was digging through my purse in search of reading glasses.

That's when I saw it, a note wedged in an inside pocket of my bag. *Was I really that careless with my purse?*

My chest tightened as I checked to make sure my wallet was still intact. When I was certain it was, I read the note silently while Coco continued to flip through the suitcase book.

My first reaction? *Oh, please.* Any man who calls a woman "first class" is a man who will also call her a "lady" and, later, a "lover." It reeked of Tom Jones and Neil Diamond.

But it was even worse than that. This guy had obviously *meant* to bump into me and ruin my blouse—a favorite Donna

Karan piece—so he could offer to pay the cleaning bill if I'd just send him my e-mail address. *What kind of scam was this?*

I tried to remember what he looked like, but it had all happened so fast. I couldn't have picked him out of a lineup.

And what *look* did I have that made me appear Parisian? Was it just the fact that I drank two bottles of wine on the flight? Two *tiny* bottles. In total, probably less than one bar-size glass of wine. *That* made me look Parisian? Oh please, Mr. Lineman.

Why were men so damn pathetic? More to the point: Why did only the most pathetic men find me attractive?

I read the note again. "Our side of the pond." Oh, stop. Who *says* that? And wait. He's "not traveling alone"?

Now I wished I had seen this guy. So he was traveling with someone (the poor girl) and sticking notes in other women's purses? Oh, this was a class act. And they say men can't multitask? Did he preprint these things before he left home, and then find lonely-looking women to spill things on so he could stick notes in their purses?

Did I *look* lonely? Answer: No. I looked tired, which I was. And I always looked more tired when I traveled. And I was using dime-store makeup because I'd run out of everything good and didn't have time to go shopping for cosmetics before we left Chicago.

I decided right then and there to treat myself to new makeup in Paris. Maybe Coco and I could get professional makeup lessons at Galeries Lafayette. That would be fun.

I considered e-mailing the note-passing joker just to let him know what a jackass he was. *No,* I thought, *what I really should do is give the note to airport security—or maybe Interpol?—and let them deal with it.* I mean, honestly, it was outrageous that this jerk had practically *assaulted* me on the plane. And then he had the audacity to rummage through my purse? *What I really should do,* I thought, *was . . .*

"Mo-om!" Coco was waving her hand in front of my face.

"What?"

"They don't have it," she said.

"Have what?"

"My *bag*," Coco stated emphatically. "It's not here."

"It has to be here," I told the woman behind the counter. Then, in broken French, I asked if it was possible the bag was on the next flight.

"You can wait if you want to," the woman finally answered, as if waiting for luggage was something people did for enjoyment. She had a silk scarf tied around her neck in that effortlessly stylish way only French women can pull off.

"Could it be stolen?" I asked.

"*Eees* possible," the woman said, looking in the distance and frowning.

Why did French women feel the need to sulk? Did they think their pouting—combined with that catty air of self-important laziness they cultivated—made them even more beautiful? The fact that it did only made it doubly annoying.

"Mom," Coco said, tears now welling in her eyes. "I need my *stuff*."

"I know," I said. Then, turning to Mademoiselle Scarf, I said firmly: "*S'il vous plait.* How do we report a missing bag? Or a *stolen* bag?"

"There," said the woman, making an airy gesture toward a

counter littered with forms against the opposite wall. "Or you can file the paperwork online. The *eeeenternet.*"

As I saw it, I had two options: one was to tell Mademoiselle Scarf that she was in the wrong line of work; the other was to breathe deeply and solve the problem myself.

I put my arm around Coco's shoulder. "Let's find an Internet café. We'll file a report with the airline."

Coco sniffled and nodded. And then, as was her habit, she ran her hands nervously through her toffee-colored hair.

My daughter. My beautiful eighteen-year-old daughter. She would throttle me if I told her in that moment she looked like her most adorable self. She would also object to the fact that I couldn't help loving these rare times when she needed me. It was such a nice change from recent years when I seemed to have become an unwanted appendage, like those absurd-looking prehensile arms on dinosaurs.

"But first, we're going to have a delicious lunch," I said.

As a chef, I have always believed that a good meal can solve most of life's problems. I slipped the creepy note in the pocket of my black slacks and forgot about it until that evening.

CHAPTER 5

Webb

I couldn't blame Dad for being pissed. He had a lot on his mind. I'd told him I'd stay out of his way on this trip. And here I was screwing up already.

We were in the hotel lobby. Dad was talking to the concierge, trying to explain the situation.

"We flew from St. Louis to Chicago," Dad began.

"Chicago," the concierge echoed. "Very *bayou*-tiful city."

"It is," agreed Dad. "And then from Chicago, we flew to Paris. And in Paris, we caught a flight here. To Madrid."

"Madrid!" said the concierge, gesturing grandly with his hands. "Welcome to Madrid!"

"Yes," Dad said, gritting his teeth. "Thank you."

This wasn't going well.

Dad's BlackBerry was chirping. He looked uncharacteristically hopeful at the interruption, and then excused himself to check his messages. I collapsed in a lobby chair with the errant duffel bag at my feet. I couldn't help looking at it dismissively, like it was a stray dog that had followed me home from school.

And that's when I saw it: a small white card tucked in a side pocket of the bag. I pulled it out and read it.

CocoChi@com

Dad was still messing with his BlackBerry and swearing under his breath. So I stuck the card in my pocket, grabbed the duffel bag, and approached the concierge.

"Um," I said. "¿Tiene una, um, sala con—"

I had no idea how to say "computer" in Spanish, so I stupidly tapped my fingers on an invisible keyboard in front of me.

The concierge responded enthusiastically. "How wonderful is your Spanish!" he said. "Yes, we have the business center. It is down the hallway. To your left."

"Gracias," I said.

I caught Dad's eye and indicated with my head where I was going. I still had the wrong bag, but at least I now had a clue who it belonged to. Something in me wanted to solve this screwup alone, without having to waste any more of Dad's time.

When I found the business center, I logged on to a computer, opened my e-mail account, and started writing.

CHAPTER 6

Coco

After we left the airport for the second time in one day—*argh*—Mom and I had lunch at a café in a neighborhood called Saint-Germain-des-Prés. We sat outside at a little round marble-top table under a blue awning. It was my first meal in Paris.

I had a plain omelet, which weirdly came with french fries. It should've tasted delicious. I should've felt chic. But instead I felt like crap because I was wearing the same clothes I'd had on the day before, when we left Chicago.

"Isn't this wonderful?" Mom asked, trying to be all bright and cheery.

I needed to be nice to Mom. She'd had a rough couple of weeks.

"Yeah, it's cool," I said. "I want to take pictures of everything." And then I remembered. "My camera's in my bag."

"You *packed* your new camera?" Mom asked. "That should've been in your carry-on."

"I didn't actually think they could lose my luggage on one friggin' flight," I said sharply. "We didn't even have a *connection*. If you'd have let me bring my iPhone, I could've taken pictures with *that*."

"Honey," Mom said firmly, "we're going to find an Internet café and report your bag to the airline."

So that's what we did. After lunch, we found an Internet café right next to an ATM where Mom got some euros. She handed me a thin stack of bills.

"Here," she said. "Put these in your pocket. Keep an eye on them."

"Mo-om! It's not my fault about the bag!"

"I didn't say it was. I'm just telling you to watch out for pickpockets."

"Right," I mumbled. My eyes were stinging. I knew if I didn't watch it, I would start crying again.

I hated when I acted bitchy with my mom. But I couldn't help it. She always knew *exactly* what to say to make me come totally unglued. And then she'd have some credible but completely random excuse about what she *really* meant, so it seemed like *I* was the one who was in the wrong.

We were barely speaking by the time we settled in at separate computer terminals.

"I'll deal with the airline," Mom said, handing me a slip of paper with a log-in password. "You do whatever you want."

Fine. I immediately went to my Facebook account. I had a few messages, which I glanced at quickly. Unlike my friends,

I found keeping up with Facebook dull and exhausting. So I opened my e-mail account. That's where I saw a message from an address I didn't recognize.

Fr: Webbn@com
To: CocoChi@com
Subject: Your bag

Dear CocoChi,

I got your e-mail from the card in your bag, which I picked up by accident this morning at the airport in Paris. I would've taken it back to the airport, but I left almost immediately for Madrid. I didn't even realize I had the wrong bag until I got to the hotel. Is there any chance you have my bag? I think I forgot to put my name on it. But you'll know it's mine if it looks exactly like your bag, except it's filled with guy stuff and a couple of books, including *Walden* by Henry David Thoreau. (A good book, if you haven't read it.)

Anyway, sorry about the mix-up. If there's anything in my bag you want to wear, help yourself. At some point I'd like to get my bag back, but I'm not sure how we're supposed to do that. Any thoughts? I will be back in Paris on Saturday and then back home in St. Louis on Sunday.

Sincerely jet-laggedly yours,
Webb Nelson

I responded immediately.

Fr: CocoChi@com
To: Webbn@com
Subject: Re: Your bag

Mr. Nelson:

Thank you SO much for letting me know you have my bag. I am HAPPY and relieved beyond words! My mom is checking the airline's website right now to figure out how we're supposed to exchange bags.

I'll get back to you soon.

Thanks for writing!

Coco Sprinkle (in Paris)

P.S. If you don't mind me asking, what kind of name is Webb ‿ (That's supposed to be a question mark, but I can't find one on this keyboard.)

CHAPTER 7

Andrew

I'd been in Madrid less than three hours, and already I was regretting taking the job.

The problem wasn't the show itself. I liked the concept. The exhibit was titled *Love in the Postdigital Age.* The idea was to showcase the first generation of artists working in a postdigital environment, artists who had come of age with PlayStations, Facebook, and iPods. Their art reflected their electronic sensibility. Instead of working with canvas and paint, these artists used interactive computer games, virtual-reality installations, laser displays, and 3-D short films.

The museum had hired me to create a space that would display these works in a way that encouraged viewers to not just see them, but, in the words of the curator, "to experience them and their creators' passion." Or what passed for passion. (Forgive the cynicism, but that's what you get when you hire a fifty-three-year-old exhibit designer.)

The curator was a woman named Solange Bartel. I'd worked with Solange on previous shows and spoken with her by phone dozens of times during the months I worked on the design for this exhibit. From the beginning, Solange was clear about her vision for the show. We agreed on the importance of creating a space that felt modern and high-tech, but not cold and uncaring. After all, this was a show about love.

I'd heard nothing but good things from Solange. For weeks, every e-mail from her was positive. But if her first message to me in Madrid was any indication, Solange was like every client I'd ever worked for. Everything is wonderful, perfect, *brilliant*—until forty-eight hours before the exhibit is scheduled to open, when everything becomes a problem, a crisis, a disaster. And it's all my fault.

"A cluster," Solange wrote in her e-mail. "No elec since last pm."

Most of the pieces in the show required monitors or plasma screens, so a power loss was clearly a problem.

"Just got to hotel 1 hr ago," I responded on my BlackBerry. "Grabbing something to eat and then I'll be @ site."

"Hurry!" she e-mailed back.

I skimmed the rest of my messages, looking for a response from Ms. 6B. Nothing. So I went in search of Webb, who had parked himself in the hotel business center.

"Hey, Dad," he said, smiling broadly. "I think I'm getting this situation figured out."

"Situation?"

"My lost bag," he said. "My clothes and stuff."

"Oh, right," I said. "Good."

This *was* good. I wanted Webb to be able to solve his own problems. Let him be resourceful, I thought. Let him find his way in the world. Let him develop the buoyancy that life demands. He was seventeen, for God's sake. Let him learn how to look people in the eye and deliver a firm handshake. And please don't let him grow up to be one of those thirty-year-old guys I always saw on flights, playing games on their phones and laptops.

"Let's get something to eat and then head over to the exhibit space," I said. "I've got a lot of work to do."

Webb hesitated. "Um, is it okay if I stay here for a while? Till I get this bag stuff figured out?"

"You're okay on your own?"

"Yeah," he said. "I can get food here at the hotel, can't I?"

"Sure."

So I went back up to the room to get my drawings and briefcase. I had three more messages from Solange. Now the air-conditioning wasn't working in the Palacio de Cristal.

"It was working y/day," she wrote. "Today = nothing. People cannot sweat like pigs @ exhibit opening!"

I assured her everything would be in working order before the opening reception on Tuesday night. And then I felt immediately exhausted by the hours of work ahead of me.

I knew I didn't have time for a real meal. I grabbed a Toblerone from the minibar and chewed it without pleasure.

Leaving the hotel, I stopped outside the business center. Webb was still sitting in front of a computer. He was eating potato chips from a plate and laughing at something on the screen. Some sort of computer game, no doubt, played with a new so-called friend in New Zealand or Hong Kong.

I paused to watch this boy I'd raised from birth. Here we were in a European capital, and he'd rather spend time in front of a computer screen. He'd rather play a damn game than walk through the streets of Madrid.

Like all parents, I attributed what I didn't like about my son to nature while crediting my nurturing skills for the traits I did like.

Webb was a sweet boy. A good person. I had no doubt of that. And as if to reassure me of this fact, Webb chose that moment to turn and look at me through the glass doors of the business center. He flashed a smile my way before happily returning to the computer.

I didn't know whether to laugh or cry.

CHAPTER 8

Daisy

I had to find Coco's bag. Either that or put up with a pouty teenager for a week.

A quick Internet search yielded the following information: If an airline loses a bag, the passenger can claim up to twenty-eight hundred dollars. But approximately 98 percent of all bags reported lost or stolen are eventually found, so passengers rarely get more than the two- or three-hundred-dollar pittance the airline provides to compensate for the hassle of a late bag.

That wasn't going to help. The camera alone was worth three hundred dollars. And I really didn't feel like schlepping back to the airport again to fill out the necessary paperwork.

I knew if I told Coco the airline would give her five hundred dollars, she'd be happy. Yes, it would mean lying to my daughter. But it would be worth it to get on with this vacation and not have to put up with her sour attitude. Besides, it'd be fun to go shopping in Paris. I could buy Coco a few nice pieces that she could take with her to college in the fall.

I liked this approach, but I wanted to mull it over for a minute before I committed myself to a five-hundred-dollar fib.

By habit, I went to my e-mail account, where I deleted the junk without reading it. I then skimmed messages from friends and former colleagues. A waiter I'd known a few years earlier had sent me a link to a newspaper article.

Chicago Tribune, Sunday, April 17
What Does Daisy Sprinkle Want?

View full text of story

I couldn't resist. I clicked on the link and read the story.

What Does Daisy Sprinkle Want?
Chicago's Favorite Chef Quits—Again

Less than a month after winning the coveted James Beard Award for Outstanding Chef, Daisy Sprinkle has left Bon Soir, the trendy French restaurant that lured her away last year from Maison Blanche, which lured her away from . . . Well, who can remember anymore?

Sprinkle's m.o. since arriving in Chicago almost two decades ago has been to flit from restaurant to restaurant, transforming each as if with fairy dust into the city's "it" place to eat. But as soon as she's succeeded—and sometimes within days of that success—Sprinkle moves on, usually without notice or, it seems, reason.

In an interview last year with *Celebrate Chicago!* magazine, Sprinkle compared her work in some of the city's finest restaurants to parenting. "Both require hard work, long hours, good luck and endless loads of laundry," quipped Sprinkle, a single mother who is known to demand in her contracts a "clean, quiet, private room in the restaurant" for her daughter to study while Sprinkle works her magic in the kitchen during the grueling 3-till-midnight dinner shift.

But the chef who has made an art of launching new restaurants has become increasingly talented at leaving them.

All of which begs the question: What does Daisy Sprinkle want? And what will it take for her to stay at one eatery long enough for us to dine there more than

I couldn't read a word more. The banality of it made my teeth hurt.

Fairy dust? Is that what they thought my secret was? *Flitting? Magic?* God help me.

If anyone ever bothered to watch me in the kitchen, they'd know my secret: I worked like a dog, especially in a new kitchen where there was an enormous amount of work to be done to establish high standards and perfect protocol. Everyone had to know what was expected and what wouldn't be tolerated.

I was best at beginnings, when I could teach my colleagues in the kitchen, as well as the waitstaff and even the owners—it was shocking how little people who owned restaurants knew about food—how it wasn't magic that produced an exquisite meal. It wasn't *fairy dust*. It was hard work. And when you did it right—that meant mastering the techniques, using the best and freshest ingredients, and having the right equipment—it was as gloriously predictable as, well, a perfect crème brûlée.

But a good meal should be surprising, too. In every dish, there should be something you can't quite identify. Something that pulls you in for another taste. That's what makes cooking an art.

And what I had said to that reporter from *Celebrate Chicago!* was that the long hours, hard work, good luck, and laundry were the *only* things cooking and parenting had in common. In all other respects cooking was the antithesis to parenting. You could do all the right things with a child, use all the best ingredients—private schools, expensive summer camps, cello lessons, chess club—and still turn out with something you wouldn't want even your closest friends to see.

Food obeyed me. I understood it. Teenage girls were a different story. As if to remind myself of this fact, I glanced over at Coco. She was typing away furiously with a wild grin on her face.

One minute she was in tears, the next she was giddy with joy. She was the most unpredictable creature on earth. But one thing was constant: she was a perfectionist, like her mother, which meant she wasn't happy when life didn't go her way.

I logged off the computer, grabbed my purse, and walked over to Coco. "Are you ready to— "

"Mo-om!" Coco shrieked.

"What?"

"You're *reading* my e-mail!"

She said it with the sense of righteous indignation she'd perfected when she learned to drive and became an expert on that and everything else.

"I promise you, I am *not* reading your e-mail," I said. I resisted the urge to tell her I couldn't give a rat's ass what petty drama was unfolding back home among her friends. (They are all very nice girls, I should note. But my God in heaven, the never-ending *drama* cultivated by these young women exhausted me on every level.)

I closed my eyes and recited the following information: "The airline will give you twenty-eight hundred dollars if they've really lost your bag. But it's more likely that they've simply *misplaced* your bag. And for that, they'll give you, uh, let's see. Five hundred dollars."

"Okay," Coco said, turning her back to me. "Actually, I need five more minutes."

"Actually, why?" I was trying to break her of this *actually* habit.

"*Moth-ur!*" she yelped. "I'm in the *middle* of something. Can't you see that?"

"Fine," I said. "I'll be outside."

As I waited, I reminded myself what Nancy, my therapist, always said. How important it was at times like these to breathe. How deep breathing really did help to slow the heart rate and prevent anxiety attacks. How simply breathing could make you feel better.

Still, I had to wonder if I'd made a major blunder in bringing Coco with me on this trip. Was her constant emotional whiplash a result of hormones? Or was it becoming who she was?

Senior prom was Saturday night, and Coco hadn't been asked. She purported not to care. "Nobody goes to those dances," she'd informed me recently. "Dating is for *losers*." But I knew many of her friends were going to the dance with dates—not in a group, as Coco had as a junior. I could only guess that this e-mail emergency concerned a friend who had recently been asked—or axed—by a boy.

Coco was a leader in her peer group. As frustrated as I was with her at the moment, I was glad she was the friend other girls could confide in. I resolved to try to be more patient with her in the name of the sisterhood.

Meanwhile, the newspaper headline waved in my brain like an enemy flag. "What Does Daisy Sprinkle Want?"

Should I make them a list? I could've rattled off a whole menu of things I wanted: Good health for my daughter and me. A fulfilling career. A comfortable home. Financial security.

Of course I wanted those things. Everybody did. The problem was, I had all of them. So what else did I want? What else were women like me supposed to want?

I looked in the window at Coco typing. Now she was laughing with her eyes closed and both hands cupped over her mouth. My daughter, the human teeter-totter.

Clearly she was in the middle of something. Is that what I

wanted? To be in the middle of something complicated and dramatic? To be a cheerleader for someone else's romance? Or to have a romance of my own?

No, thanks. I'd done that. I'd been doing that for years. The last time was a year and two restaurants ago. (Or was it two years and three restaurants ago? Time flies when you're not having sex.) In any case, it was with the owner of a French restaurant in Oak Park who had convinced me to leave a bistro in the Loop. The guy, Chuck ("Why were you even *taking* calls from a man named Chuck?" my friend Solange later demanded), insisted he couldn't live without me and my *poulet roti l'ami Louis,* otherwise known as roast chicken. For what it's worth, any moron can make it. You just rub a chicken with poultry fat—goose fat is best, but chicken fat will do— before roasting.

I stupidly took a job at Chuck's restaurant and more stupidly started dating Chuck—only to be told by a waiter six months later that I was just a side dish. The hostess (the hostess!) was his entrée. And, oh yes, I also learned that Chuck was married to a woman who lived in New York.

Solange put it best: *Chuck that.*

So what *did* I want? Another ridiculous and humiliating relationship? No. Another seventy-hour-a-week job? No. Not yet, anyway.

I wanted to visit museums and lose myself in art for a glorious week. I wanted to eat fabulous food for seven whole days without worrying about price points or profit margins. I wanted to spend time with my daughter without the interruption of cell phones—hers or mine. Some new Chanel makeup would be nice. Shoes? Only if I found a pair I couldn't live without. Clothes? I could always use another silk blouse or two and some lovely new underwear.

It was settled, then. During our week in Paris we'd shop, museum hop, and dine in the finest restaurants. And that, right there, was the answer to the question posed by the headline. *Never mind what Daisy Sprinkle wants*, I thought. *I know I need a small vacation.*

Was that so much to ask?

CHAPTER 9

Webb

I was responding to her first message when I got her second:

Fr: CocoChi@com
To: Webbn@com
Subject: Re: Your bag

Hello again. Mr. Nelson.

My mom has done a little research and says the airline will reimburse $2.800 for a lost or stolen bag and $500 for a late bag—that is. one that's delivered to a passenger days after he/she arrives.

Your thoughts ‿ (Still can't find the question mark on this keyboard. I miss my iPhone. Sad....)

Coco Sprinkle

I liked girls who were polite and sort of stiff like this. I could tell without even seeing her that the gypsy blouse was all wrong for her.

I also liked that she thought that I was a mister. Had she really not looked inside my bag and seen that I was a teenager? It didn't seem possible.

I wiped the potato chip grease from my hands onto my jeans and fired off a response.

Fr: Webbn@com
To: CocoChi@com
Subject: Re: Re: Your bag
Attached: Keyboard conversion download

Okay, Mizz Sprinkle. Fess up. Have you really not examined the contents of my bag closely enough to realize I'm not a Mr.? Or are you just being polite?

For the record, I'm 17 years old. I live in St. Louis. I'm an Aquarius.

My name, you ask? It's my sadistic dad's tribute to his favorite songwriter, Jimmy Webb. Need I tell you what my nickname was in elementary school? Charlotte.

(And if you think my first name's bad, my middle name's even worse: Gaudí. My dad's favorite architect is Antoni Gaudí.)

But back to the business at hand: $2800 for a missing bag? Cool. And no wonder all the airlines are going broke. A person more evil than I (or me?) might suggest we file claims for stolen bags, pocket the money, and then exchange the bags when we get home by UPS or FedEx—whichever's cheaper.

It'd sorta be like *Strangers on a Train*. Have you ever seen that movie? Two guys who don't know each other meet on a train. (You probably could've figured that out from the title.) Anyway, they start talking about how they have these difficult people in their lives. And one guy (who turns out to be a crackpot) suggests they kill each other's problem person because no one would suspect a guy of killing someone he didn't know. It gets better from there.

Of course I'm not a crackpot. Or a murderer. Or a bag thief. How 'bout you?

Webb

P.S. Sounds like you're using a European-Arabic keyboard. I'll attach a keyboard conversion file for your convenience.

P.P.S. For the record, I'm cell free this week, too. Left it in my locker on Friday.

CHAPTER 10

Coco

Mom was giving me the skunk eye from the sidewalk, so I had to write fast:

Fr: CocoChi@com
To: Webbn@com
Subject: Re: Re: Re: Your bag

Webb,

Thanks for that converter file. I can now ask questions with a?b?a?n?d?o?n.

I can't believe you've seen *Strangers on a Train*. I wrote a paper on that book/movie for my Art of Film class last year. It's such an elegantly crafted story. Did you know Patricia Highsmith also wrote the Talented Mr. Ripley books, which were made into movies? Totally worth seeing, if you haven't already.

As for *Walden*, we read that last year in English. I liked it a lot until I learned that li'l Henry went home to his mother's house for lunch most days. And didn't his aunt have to bail his butt out of jail? Hmm.

Now, about your idea of "stealing" each other's bags: You are one clever lad. And I hate to sound like a total drip, but … I'm trying to get into an honors college program, and I need a luggage-stealing charge on my record like I need herpes. So what do you think about just finding a way to exchange bags when we get home? I live in Chicago (that's the CHI in my e-mail). My mom and I fly back on Saturday. (That's this coming Saturday, six days from now.)

In the meantime, I'm all for taking the $500. You should, too. This IS an inconvenience, after all. (No offense to you or your clothes.)

Gotta go. Never heard of Antoni Gaudí. I'll Google him when I have more time. Right now my mom's standing on the sidewalk, tapping her foot, and glaring at me. Roll on, graduation....

Euros truly.
Coco (We could talk at length about sadistic parents and how they name their children) Sprinkle

P.S. Almost forgot: I only peeked in your bag long enough to know it wasn't mine!

P.P.S. Hey, the left-the-cell-in-my-locker line is cute. But how do I know you're not really some creepy 50-year-old international playboy trying to chat up a high school girl? Answer at your leisure. I probly won't be able to check e-mail till tmw.

Andrew

The exhibit was at the Palacio de Cristal, also known as the Crystal Palace, in the center of Retiro Park. The building itself was gorgeous. Built in 1887 to showcase exotic flora and fauna from the Philippines, then a Spanish colony, the Crystal Palace still felt like an imperial greenhouse with a fanciful domed roof.

But all that natural light made it the exact *wrong* place to stage a postmodern exhibit that relied heavily on darkness. How were visitors supposed to see the digital images on the screens and monitors? Plus, someone had neglected to notice that the Crystal Palace wasn't exactly rainproof. The roof included several spans of mesh screen for air circulation. Fortunately, it didn't look like rain. But it was one more thing to worry about.

I was never invited to serve on site selection committees.

My job always began after a venue, usually the wrong venue, had been chosen. My challenge, then, was to design temporary rooms—walls, ceilings, lighting grids—to display a particular exhibit to its best advantage.

For this show I'd designed a dome within the already domed Crystal Palace to create a more intimate space. Even with that, I'd still had to devise a system of electronic blinds for the windows that would block out the exterior light.

Much of my job was monkey work. I always subcontracted out anything that involved running cables or hanging drywall. But I saved for myself the job of placing art. To my mind, that was the most important part of any job. If I had any talent at all, it was knowing where to put things.

It was an instinct, I guess, this ability to know where something belonged, how it fit in with the whole, why it belonged in one place and not another. I suppose that's why I'd felt compelled to hide the note in Ms. 6B's bag. It belonged there. *I* belonged with her.

Okay, so maybe I didn't. Maybe that's why she hadn't responded to my invitation to strike up an e-acquaintance. I was still trying to shake off her rejection as I walked through Retiro Park.

When I finally arrived at the Crystal Palace, I saw a dozen grim-faced men in coveralls, marching in and out of the building with armloads of cables and power tools. Solange was standing inside, dead center in the middle of the antiquated greenhouse.

She was a small woman—I bet she didn't weigh a hundred

pounds—but feisty as hell. She was close to sixty years old and still the most sought-after freelance curator in Europe. Museum boards paid her hefty sums to put together temporary shows intended to generate a lot of revenue and good publicity. We'd worked together on several shows. I respected her enormously—and liked her, too, except when she was on a tear, which she clearly was when I arrived.

Instead of the traditional kiss on both cheeks, Solange welcomed me with a barrage of complaints.

"The electronic window shades are stuck," she began, clicking a remote device repeatedly as if to demonstrate its futility. "You said they would go up and down. Up at night when it is dark outside. Down during the day so people can see the exhibits. They are not working."

"We can fix that," I said, rubbing my neck. I was sore from the hours I'd spent on the plane, craning my neck to see Ms. 6B.

"And the circuits, *pouf!* They keep blowing," Solange continued with her signature staccato delivery.

"I'll take a look at—" I started to say.

"And the caterer called," she went on. "His father died."

"That's terrible."

"He cannot make food for the opening reception. Oh, and there is a bad smell in the lavatories. And—"

It was no use. Solange didn't want to discuss the situation. She wanted to vent. At me. So I let her, making sure to nod from time to time. The song "Wichita Lineman" started to play in my head.

I am a lineman for the county and I drive the main road
Searchin' in the sun for another overload.
I hear you singin' in the wire, I can hear you through
the whine
And the Wichita Lineman is still on the line.

I know I need a small vacation but it don't look like
rain.
And if it snows that stretch down south won't ever stand
the strain.
And I need you more than want you, and I want you
for all time.
And the Wichita Lineman is still on the line.

I'd always loved that Jimmy Webb song. The image of a guy driving down a county road, longing for someone, had always resonated with me. And the line about needing more than wanting? It never failed to break my heart, even though I wasn't exactly sure what it meant.

Truth was, I'd never fully understood the song. Who was he listening to? Why was he still on the line? I'd never known. But to me this song represented art. It begged questions. It packed an emotional punch. There was a tension between the parts of the song I understood and the parts I didn't. Plus, there was the necessary touch of sadness that all true art demanded. The ache of living and the comfort of love: that's what I heard in "Wichita Lineman."

As Solange talked, I looked around at the postdigital

nonsense trying to pass itself off as art. The most prominent installation was called *Spin the Cell Phone*. The artist had created an interactive obstacle course designed to replicate the art of finding love via texting.

Who were these artists? Had they ever been in love? These were people who would prefer to sit in front of a computer rather than under a tree with another human being. People who had no idea what it meant to drive along a county road, yearning for someone. People, I hated to admit, very much like my own son.

Solange had stopped talking.

"Are you even *listening*?" she asked, her balled fists wedged against her bony hips.

"Yes," I said. "We should . . . um . . . We should maybe consider . . ."

"What?" she inquired. "What should we consider?"

"We should consider sending flowers to the caterer," I said. "For his father's funeral. Let's do that. And then we'll get this other stuff sorted out."

"Listen to me," she said, shaking a skinny finger in my face. "The opening reception is in two days. I am not telling you how to do your job. I am simply telling you what your job *is*. And that is to have everything *à la perfection* when the doors open on Tuesday night."

And with that, she marched off.

CHAPTER 12

Daisy

Maybe it was the lunch. Or the thought of a five-hundred-dollar shopping spree. Or the fact that she'd had a chance to connect with her friends in the Internet café. I didn't know, and I didn't have to know. I was just glad to see Coco grinning when she joined me on the sidewalk.

"Thanks for waiting," she said. "Oh, Mom. Look!"

We were standing in front of Cour du Commerce Saint-André, a lovely cobblestone passageway. It was at number 9 that Dr. Joseph-Ignace Guillotin allegedly perfected the decapitating device.

"Believe it or not, Dr. Guillotin was opposed to the death penalty," I told Coco. "He hoped the guillotine, which he didn't invent by the way, would replace more gruesome forms of execution, like hanging. And that it might be the first step to abolishing executions altogether."

Coco stared at the building. "Actually, I would love a picture of that. I wish I had my camera. Or my phone."

I could feel my chest tightening. Were we *actually* going to spend the whole week lamenting every missed photo op? If so, I would need an appointment with Dr. Guillotin.

"But it's not like this is the *only* time I'll ever be on this street in my whole life," she countered, as if reading my mind. "I should write about it. Or sketch it—with colored pencils. I bet I'd get extra credit in French class."

"That's a *great* idea," I said. "I'm sure we can find colored pencils. We're in Paris, the city of art and artists."

"And executioners!" Coco said, laughing wickedly and tucking her arm through mine.

"Don't be too hard on Dr. Guillotin," I cautioned. "He was a humanitarian and a reformist. Executions in his day were public spectacles and almost unimaginably brutal. That's what he was fighting against."

"Oh, I just love gruesome stuff like this," Coco purred, pulling me closer. "Let's wander around and look at everything creepy and cool."

And we did. The entire afternoon.

We should've been back at Solange's apartment, taking naps and trying to shake off our jet lag. This was still our arrival day. But it felt wonderful to wander the narrow streets, admiring the beauty that enveloped us.

Hours later, when we weren't hungry for dinner, we decided to get some pastries to take back to the apartment. We chose a patisserie based on the spellbinding window display of pastel meringues stacked with architectural precision.

"The French know how to do sweets like nobody else," I told Coco. It was the reason I'd studied in Paris twenty years earlier. I was heartened that I could still remember most of the names of the delicacies: *opéra, tropizenne, castel, mille-feuilles, éclair au chocolat ou café.*

"Mom, what do you want?" Coco asked when we were inside.

"Hmm," I said, mulling over the possibilities. The *tartes des pommes* looked lovely. So fresh and light and unlike the morbidly heavy Death by Chocolate monstrosities I saw on too many American menus.

"Mom, what do you *want*?" Coco repeated.

And with that question, the spell was broken. Because instead of delighting in the edible art in front of my eyes, I was remembering that idiotic headline in the *Chicago Tribune*.

"What do I want?" I asked, feeling my blood pressure rising. "I want people to stop asking me what the hell I want."

I caught myself. *Don't take your frustrations out on Coco,* I could hear Nancy the wonder therapist telling me. *Anxiety is unexpressed anger. Breathe deeply. Are you angry at Coco?* No. *But you are angry. Who are you angry with?* I'm not angry, I'm just tired. I need a small vacation.

I took a deep breath and tried again. "I'm sorry, sweetie. I want whatever you're having."

Coco smiled mysteriously and ordered a small, hideous-looking thing called *séduction.*

CHAPTER 13

Webb

D ad was going to be busy with work stuff for hours, so I could've responded to Coco's message right away. But that would've seemed lame, especially given her "Answer at your leisure" suggestion. Wasn't that code for "Dude, don't e-mail me for a while"?

I logged off and left the hotel. The concierge was still at his post. He smiled and lifted his chin at me.

"Luego," I said with a wave. I felt like a dope using my crappy high school Spanish. But it seemed ruder to expect everyone in the world to speak English.

It was six o'clock Madrid time. Eleven o'clock St. Louis time. I'd been in the same clothes for twenty-four hours. I knew I needed a shower, but it felt good to be outside in the fresh air.

I liked Madrid. Dad had brought me with him twice before on work trips. We'd stayed both times at the Palace Hotel, so I was familiar with the neighborhood. Standing outside the hotel, I could look to my right and see the fountain with Neptune and his seahorses. The Prado Museum was just down the street. So was Retiro Park, home of the Crystal Palace, which sounds like a casino, but it's more like a huge antique terrarium that'd been converted into a museum. That's the place Dad was working, and where I was headed when I left the hotel.

I walked down Paseo del Prado, losing myself to the sights, sounds, and dense magic of the city. There's something weirdly calming about being alone in a big city. It made me feel like the universe was hugely generous, and that my species was so damn smart to have constructed such a beautiful city. If it were up to me, we'd still be living in huts and roasting meat over an open fire.

I remembered a recent conversation I'd had with Dad. He asked if I'd thought about what I might like to study in college. He wanted to know if I had any careers in mind. I told him I'd love to be a modern-day caveman. He almost started crying, poor guy. Parents have it so hard these days.

I wandered for an hour or so, feeling freakishly tall among the *Madrileños*. After a while, I discovered I'd made a giant loop and was back at the hotel. I wandered through the marble lobby and back to the business center. Once again I had the whole place to myself. I settled in and started writing.

Fr: Webbn@com
To: CocoChi@com
Subject: Re: Re: Re: Re: Your bag

Proof I am not an old creep and/or a globe-trotting internat'l playboy:

1. I have no hair growing out of my nose or ears.
2. I rarely begin sentences with "You should . . ."
3. Almost everything I own comes from either Goodwill or the Salvation Army store. (Exception: my Chuck Taylors.)
4. I've never written a real letter that requires a stamp.
5. I don't think *Casablanca* is a masterpiece.
6. Or *It's a Wonderful Life.*
7. Or *The Wizard of Oz.*

But I do love Hitchcock movies. And the Mississippi River. And the St. Louis Arch. Have you ever seen it? The official name is the Gateway Arch, but nobody in St. Louis calls it that. It's just the Arch. It was designed by an architect named Eero Saarinen. The cool thing about the Arch is that it stands 630 feet tall and is 630 wide at its base. On nights when the moon is full, it knocks you out.

But back to your question (which was delightfully sassy, I might add): One way that I *might* be confused with an old guy is my musical taste, which runs mainly toward older stuff. I have a thing for Nick Drake, Elliott Smith, Kurt Cobain—all those genius singer-songwriters who wrote brilliant songs and then killed themselves.

"What's with this sad sack and all his talk of double murder plots and suicide?" Miss Sprinkle asks herself, stepping away from the computer slowly.

Don't worry. I'm harmless.

OK, your turn now. Prove to me you're not some 45-year-old transcontinental cougar who pours herself into her daughter's jeans and looks great from the back—until she turns around and reveals her shriveled-up dried apple face, like that freaky scene from *Lost Horizon*. Another cool movie, btw.

Webb

CHAPTER 14

Coco

Back at the apartment Mom brewed a pot of hot tea while I enjoyed my pastry.

"Ready for bed?" Mom asked. She was paging through a stack of Solange's art magazines.

"It's only eight o'clock," I said. "I'm not at all tired."

Actually, I was exhausted. I hadn't slept much on the flight. Plus, I'd spotted an Internet café at the end of Solange's block.

"Can we take a walk?" I asked. "I need to check my e-mail."

"Are we going to spend our entire vacation in cybercafés?" Mom said, not looking up from her magazine.

"No, but I really need to check on someone."

So we walked down the street and reserved twenty minutes on two terminals that faced each other. I signed on to my account and read Webb's message. Then I started writing.

Fr: CocoChi@com
To: Webbn@com
Subject: Re: Re: Re: Re: Re: Your bag

Dear Mr. Superficial,

Have you ever seen *The Graduate*? If so, you'd know
from witnessing Anne Bancroft (goddess) just how 100%
GORGEOUS older women can be. But no, I'm not a cougar.
You require proof? Okay, here goes.

Unlike my mother and her friends, I fail to see the attraction
of Brad Pitt. Or George Clooney. Or Will Smith. However, I think
Sean Connery and Denzel Washington are hot hot hot, even
though they're ancient. And I'm totally in love with Clark Gable
and Gregory Peck, even though they're dead.

Further proof that I'm only 18: My clothes are stylish
(sorta) but cheaply made. My mother, by contrast,
wears pseudo-stylish sexy librarian clothes, like $250
silk blouses. Granted, everything she wears she's had
for years. So maybe it pays off in the long run. Still,
you should see how she freaks whenever she spills
something on herself or pulls a random thread from one
of her favorite "pieces," as she calls them.

Speaking of fashion, it might interest you to know that
I'm wearing your white oxford cloth shirt even as I write

these words. Don't worry. I'm going shopping tomorrow with my $500 airline money.

Yes, I've seen the Arch. It's totally cool. In fact, I was in St. Louis a month ago. I had a second interview at Washington University. I've been accepted there for next fall, but I'm trying to get into an honors program. (Did I already mention this? If so, sorry. It's on my to-stress-about list.)

Hope you're having mucho fun in Madrid.

Adios, amigo.
Coco

P.S. Oh, here's one way I'm sort of a lady geezer: As much as I miss my phone and texting, I don't really mind using e-mail. It's retro cool and vaguely Victorian, y'know? Plus, you can add groovy things, like P.S.

Two minutes later, I had a response:

Fr: Webbn@com
To: CocoChi@com
Subject: Re: Re: Re: Re: Re: Re: Your bag

Agreed. Texting is for monosyllabic morons. I don't really do it that much. Mainly b/c I lose my c/phone a lot. But wait: You're planning to go to college in STL? I want to go to Northwestern. That's your 'hood, sí? And you're wearing my white shirt? That's *muy* odd. Because I'm wearing your gypsy blouse. Olé!

Fr: CocoChi@com
To: Webbn@com
Subject: Re: Re: Re: Re: Re: Re: Re: Your bag

Dog! Are you pawing through my clothes? (Btw: It's not a gypsy blouse. It's a *peasant* blouse.)

Fr: Webbn@com
To: CocoChi@com
Subject: Re: Re: Re: Re: Re: Re: Re: Re: Your bag

Peasant blouse. Gotcha. And no pawing here. The saucy thing just flew out of the bag and wrapped itself around me, like I was Gregory Peck. I have that effect on blouses.

(You know I'm kidding, right? Are you mad? Do you think we should start seeing other people? I hope not. Because I was just thinking how cool it'd be to meet you.)

Fr: CocoChi@com
To: Webbn@com
Subject: Re: Re: Re: Re: Re: Re: Re: Re: Re: Your bag

Are you serious? About meeting?

Fr: Webbn@com
To: CocoChi@com
Subject: Re: Re: Re: Re: Re: Re: Re: Re: Re: Re: Your bag

Si. Muy serioso!
I'd love to show you around STL.
Wearing matching peasant blouses, of course.

It was all I could do to keep from howling. Why didn't my school have any guys like this who were smart and funny and who could write complete sentences? I wondered what he looked like. He seemed like a bum from the way he packed his bag. But maybe he was just rumpled in a totally adorable sheepdog way.

I wanted to ask if he had a MySpace page or was on Facebook, but that would be a total giveaway that I wanted to know what he looked like. And here I'd just called him Mr. Superficial.

So I fired off something just to keep the conversation alive.

Fr: CocoChi@com
To: Webbn@com
Subject: Re: Re: Re: Re: Re: Re: Re: Re: Re: Re: Re: Your bag

 P/blouses. Of course!

His next message to me arrived at the same second.

Fr: Webbn@com
To: CocoChi@com
Subject: Re: Re: Re: Re: Re: Re: Re: Re: Re: Re: Re: Re:
Your bag

 Hey, do you tweet or do FB or any of that crapola? I
don't. Just thought I'd mention it so you don't waste time
looking for me. I did FB for a while. But it was so much
work. Seemed too much like a job, y'know?

Fr: CocoChi@com
To: Webbn@com
Subject: Re: Re: Re: Re: Re: Re: Re: Re: Re: Re: Re: Re: Your bag

 IKR? It starts to feel like an obligation. Who needs that?
We have a lot in common, Spidey.

Fr: Webbn@com
To: CocoChi@com
Subject: Re: Re: Re: Re: Re: Re: Re: Re: Re: Re: Re: Re: Re: Your bag

   Spidey?

Fr: CocoChi@com
To: Webbn@com
Subject: Re: Re: Re: Re: Re: Re: Re: Re: Re: Re: Re: Re: Re: Re: Your bag

   Spidey = short for Spiderman = He who spins a Web(b).

Fr: Webbn@com
To: CocoChi@com
Subject: Re: Re: Re: Re: Re: Re: Re: Re: Re: Re: Re: Re: Re: Re: Your bag

   Ah, she's a witty girl. Me like.
   Okay, gotta sign off. My dad wants to go to dinner.
   Later, Blouse Girl.

Wow. I needed to digest this back at Solange's apartment, where I could think.

"Mom, are you ready?" I asked.

"Give me five minutes," she said. "I've got some business to take care of."

CHAPTER 15

Andrew

What a day. The only good news was that Webb told me he'd tracked down his bag, but probably wouldn't get it until we returned home. It didn't matter. He could pick out some new clothes in Madrid, if I could ever tear him away from the hotel business center.

I probably shouldn't have brought him along. He would've been happier spending his spring break at home with friends. Just as I was feeling grateful that he'd always managed to make nice friends, my BlackBerry signaled a new message.

Fr: Solange@com
To: Lineman@com
Subject: Today

Andrew: Thank you for your hard work today. We will have everything perfect by Tuesday, yes?

I was starting to respond when I received another message.

Fr: DaisyS@com
To: Lineman@com
Subject: FYI

Seat 13C: I found the note you placed in my bag
without my knowledge or permission. Normally I
wouldn't respond to such a sophomoric prank, but I
feel compelled to tell you how offensive I found your
gesture, given the fact that you were traveling with
someone else. I hope for her sake she wasn't aware of
your little note-passing hijinx—or the fact that you
were trying to pick up at least one woman (who knows
how many other notes you tucked away in women's
purses) on the flight from Chicago to Paris.

You wrote in your note that I am "first class." I
didn't have the opportunity to see you, but I can tell
from your behavior exactly what you are: a first-class
ASS. If you contact me again, I will inform the airline
of your unwanted, unappreciated, and completely
unacceptable behavior.

CHAPTER 16

Daisy

*I*t felt good to get that off my chest. Nancy was right. Better to express anger at the guilty party than keep it inside and let it fester until it becomes anxiety.

"C'mon, Mom, let's go," Coco said.

"Just a sec," I said.

A new message had arrived from one of my oldest friends in the world, the woman whose apartment Coco and I were borrowing.

Fr: Solange@com
To: DaisyS@com
Subject: A favor, please

Bon soir, Daisy!

   I hope by now you and Coco have settled in, yes? Please let me know if you cannot find something you need—or if you have forgotten how the shower works, etc. I stocked the refrig with your favorites (the cheese you call "slinky" is in the green glass container) and left an extra key on the desk for Coco. Did you find it? I wish I could be there to welcome you properly, but I am up to my eyebrows with this Madrid job.

This is why I am writing to you. I called the apartment several times today, but either you are not there (possible) or you are not taking my calls. (You are always the wonderful guest!) But I really need to talk with you. I will not go into details about what a f/ing mess this job has become. But everything has turned to *merde* in the final moment. I have technical problems, artistic problems, angry board members . . . and just today I learned the caterer I hired for the opening gala (Tuesday night) is cancelling because of a death in the family. Do you see where this is leading?

Daisy, chére, I am begging you (and yes, I know how desperate that sounds, but . . .), yes, BEGGING you to come to Madrid on Tuesday morning and cook. I do not care what you make. I do not care how you make it. I only need to feed 250 of Madrid's most important art patrons. Can you help me? Not a full meal. Just hors d'oeuvres. Sweet or savory. You decide. Think about this, please, and call my cell phone. The number is on the desk.

Of course the museum will pay for your services, plus travel and hotel expenses for you and Coco. Did I mention that I am desperate?

Hopelessly devoted,
xx Solange

Merde, indeed. I was looking forward to a relaxing week in Paris. But Solange was a dear friend. I met her the year I lived in Paris. I was twenty-six and attending culinary school. She was forty, which seemed ancient to me at the time, and studying art.

Solange was the second person, besides me, to know I was pregnant with Coco. When I told her the news over a weepy, two-bottle-of-wine dinner, she gave me three orders: *Stop drinking. Stop smoking. Stop feeling sorry for yourself.* She also told me, as only a forty-year-old childless woman could tell a twenty-six-year-old pregnant and unmarried friend, that she regretted only the things she hadn't done in her life, not the things she had.

More than anyone else, it was because of Solange that I became a mother. (Well, Solange and Coco's father, of course.) It was the best decision I ever made—not just having a baby, but raising Coco on my own. I had the luxury of making enough money to do so, of course. But I also had the constitution to be a single parent. It was so much easier this way. No compromises or competing parenting styles. No anger at having to assume more than my share of the parental responsibilities. Only on rare occasions did I envy my married friends. Christmas mornings and Father's Day. That was it.

I printed Solange's e-mail. Walking back to the apartment, I read it to Coco.

"I hate to let her down," I said. "But then again—"

"Mom," Coco interrupted, "we should *totally* help her out on this."

"Really? You wouldn't mind going to Madrid?"

"No!" she said. "Actually, it's *fine*."

I let the "actually" go.

"Honey," I said, "it would cut into our Paris time. We might not have a chance to do all the things you—"

Coco stopped walking. "Mother," she said, grabbing the e-mail printout from my hand and holding it in front of my face. "You don't understand. We *have* to do this."

CHAPTER 17

Webb

When I woke up the next morning, I found a note from Dad.

> Had to get an early start. Call when you
> wake up.

He left a local number, which I assumed was the Crystal Palace. I dialed the number from the phone on the nightstand.

"Dígame," said the person on the other end of the line.

"Uh, puedo hablar con Andrew Nelson, por favor?" I asked, feeling like an idiot.

"Quien?"

"El americano," I explained. "Muy grande americano."

In trying to describe my father, I sounded like I was ordering coffee. But it worked.

"Sí, sí," replied the voice on the phone.

"Hello," Dad said a minute later.

"Hey, it's me."

"Everything okay?" he asked. "I was beginning to worry."

"Yeah. I didn't even hear you leave this morning."

"Good," Dad replied. "Do you want me to come back to the hotel and get you? Or you could walk over here. You remember the way, don't you? Whatever you want to do."

I wanted to check my e-mail, but I couldn't tell him that.

"I'll come over there," I said.

"Okay, grab some breakfast first at the hotel," Dad said. "Charge it to the room. And then ask the concierge to draw you a map of how to get here, just in case. Be sure to tip him. I left some euros on the table for you."

I saw the pile of bills on the table. Then I spotted my dirty clothes in a heap on the floor.

"My clothes are going to get pretty ripe this week," I said.

"Don't worry. Everyone's in work clothes here. But we'll get the clothes situation sorted out later today. See you when you get here."

We hung up. I liked that Dad trusted me to get myself to the museum. Then again, there's a fine line between being trusted and being ignored. I often wondered if Dad planned our vacations around his work schedule so he could avoid spending long stretches of time with me. Then I felt guilty for second-guessing Dad's motivations. He really did the best he could, which wasn't half bad, considering how old he was. He was a single dad way back before it was the hipster thing to do. And he never once complained about having to raise me without any help from my mom. But he did manage to see her most Saturdays—without me.

I got dressed and stuck the euros in my pocket. When I got downstairs to the lobby, I saw my concierge *amigo*. He greeted me with a hearty "Buenos dias."

"Hey, buenos dias to you, too," I said. "So, donde está la . . ."

I couldn't remember how to say restaurant so I made the universal sign for a person feeding himself with an invisible fork. I'd always felt a weird repulsion to mimes. Now I was becoming one.

"Ah! La restaurante," the concierge sang, pointing down a hallway. "Está por allí."

"Gracias," I said, fully intending to follow Dad's instructions. But I couldn't resist stopping first at the business center to check e-mail. I smiled when I saw that I had a message from Coco.

Fr: CocoChi@com
To: Webbn@com
Subject: About your bag

Bon Jour. Mssr. Spidey.

Interesting news here. My mom and I are traveling
to (wait for it) Madrid tomorrow. It's a long story. but
she's going to cook for a friend. (My mom's a chef. Have
I already mentioned that?) Anyway. we'll fly to Madrid
early tomorrow morning and return to Paris the next day.

So we'll only be there for one night. But one night is one night, right? I was wondering if you'd like to:

a) meet

b) exchange suitcases

c) enjoy a café and/or some tapas (yummy)

d) see a bullfight (please say no!)

e) rescue a bull from a bullfight (Sí! Sí! Sí!)

f) all of the above

g) none of the above

Think about it and LMK, okay?

Hopelessly devoted,
Coco

P.S. I'm wearing your SOMEONE STILL LOVES YOU BORIS YELTSIN T-shirt. (Is that a band—or a joke?) Don't worry. I'm going shopping later today. My clothes-borrowing ways will soon be a distant memory.

CHAPTER 18

Coco

I felt a little guilty stealing Solange's "Hopelessly devoted" line. But I liked how it sounded funny and silly and a tiny bit flirty.

I sent the message from the Internet café after telling Mom that I wanted to get some croissants for breakfast. She said fine. She had a phone date with Solange, her friend and my godmother.

When I got back to the apartment, Mom was still on the phone, rattling off a list of things she needed: two stoves, twenty cookie sheets, a driver who could take her shopping, a translator, blah blah blah.

I put a croissant on a plate and slid it in front of her. She barely noticed.

"That's right. Gas stovetop and electric oven," she was saying. "And I'd really like an oven thermometer, if you can track one down."

I tuned her out as I tore off a piece of croissant and started eating. *How crazy would it be to meet this Webb guy in Madrid? And how was I ever going to explain him to my mom?*

I watched her talk on the phone while I waited for Solange's electric teakettle to heat up. Mom was wearing her sexy librarian glasses, but her eyes were closed. She was rubbing her forehead with her free hand.

"No, no, no," she said. "You don't owe me anything. Solange, please. This is what I *do*. It's not a big deal at all. All right? Okay? Don't worry. We love you, too. See you tomorrow morning."

She hung up the phone and sighed dramatically. It was her "My life is so complicated and important" sigh, but I knew in her heart of hearts she was thrilled by this new development. My mother thrives on coming to other people's rescue, especially if it can be accomplished with food. Watching her expression as she talked to Solange reminded me of how she looked when I was a kid and she brought my lunch to school on the rare days I forgot it. It made her feel like a good mom.

I know I should try harder to make her feel necessary in my life. It totally freaked her when I said I didn't need her anymore. But isn't that the whole point of growing up? A healthy bird can fly the nest? Roots and wings and all that Hallmarky crap?

"I got a croissant for you," I said, blowing on my tea. "Hope it's the right kind."

"Let me see," she said, inspecting the roll with her eagle eye. She took a bite. "Oh yes, this is good. Flaky, not chewy."

As she pulled apart her croissant, she continued to worry aloud about the Madrid event, telling me all the things she could bake and wondering which would be best.

"Do we still have time to shop for clothes today?" I asked, picking at the crumbs on my plate.

"Sure," she said. "You'll need something to wear in Madrid."

No kidding! I need to look freakin' fantastic.

After we were both showered, we took the Metro to Galeries Lafayette, which is this totally cool department store with a colored-glass domed roof. It feels like you're shopping inside a Tiffany lamp.

I hadn't realized how seriously the French take fashion. Women get dressed up, even just to go shopping, which made me feel like a complete bum given the fact that I was on day three of my jeans.

"Let's start on the third floor," Mom said as we studied the store directory.

Of course that's where she wanted to start. That's where all the fancy schmancy designer stuff was.

As soon as we got off the escalator, Mom stopped to admire an Anne Fontaine black silk blouse. She grabbed a cream-colored blouse, too.

"I thought we were shopping for *me*," I said. I didn't mean for it to come out snotty, but it did.

"We are," Mom replied, carrying the blouses on hangers in front of her. "C'mon. Let's get some lovely underthings."

The lingerie department on the third floor of Galeries Lafayette was as big as two or three Victoria's Secret stores.

But instead of teenyboppers giggling over cheesy Wonderbras and fake-out foam jobs, this place was filled with old ladies—like in their thirties and forties and fifties—buying silk bras, underwear, and weird-ass garter things.

"Here," Mom said, handing me a midnight-blue bra. "Try this on. Oh, and this one's nice, too. See if it fits. And this is pretty. Try this. And this . . ."

I slunk back to the fitting room. Before I even had my (or, actually Webb's) shirt off, a saleslady was poking and prodding me.

"American?" she asked.

"Oui," I answered. I tried to think how I could avoid undressing in front of this woman. "Um, comment dit-on . . . ?"

"No, no," she said, waving away my question with her hand. "This you must try on. There is no other way."

So I did. I tried on at least twenty-five bras. There's something funny about shopping in Paris. The women who work in stores will absolutely *not* let you buy something, not even a bra, unless it fits perfectly and looks great on you, which was half humiliating but half helpful, too. I walked out of that dressing room with three of the most beautiful silk bras I'd ever seen in my life, along with matching underwear.

"This place is amazing," I told Mom, who'd also picked up some silky stuff for herself.

"Didn't I tell you?" she said in her singsongy voice. "Do you know how much French women spend on lingerie?"

"Mother," I hissed as we were getting on the escalator. "People can hear you."

"Women in France spend twenty percent of their clothing

budget on underwear," she continued, undeterred. "Now do you understand why I told you to pack your worst bras and undies? I always do that when I come here. That way you can wear your old stuff once, throw it away, and replace it with prettier pieces."

"Keep in mind I don't *have* any underwear to throw away because I don't have my bag, remember?"

"Well," Mom said, pointing to my shopping bag filled with bras and matching underwear, "now you have some lovely new things to wear."

We took the escalator down to the second floor, home of Mode Tendance, which I translated as cool clothes that were hipper than the designer stuff on the third floor.

Mom and I both found things we liked and retreated to side-by-side dressing rooms. I was trying on jeans with short, fitted jackets. I decided maybe in Madrid I'd wear a jacket with a camisole under it, if I could find one in Solange's closet. Would that look cool or slutty? I wanted to wear something super Euro chic when I met Webb.

"Do you think Solange would let me borrow a scarf to wear with this?" I asked Mom, showing off my jeans, T-shirt, and linen jacket ensemble.

"Sure," Mom said. "Turn around. That jacket looks great on you. Would you wear it back home?"

"Of course!" I insisted, unsure if I really would or not.

"Linen wrinkles like crazy," Mom warned.

"Wrinkles are cool," I claimed. "I could totally wear this to school next year. And I've got five hundred dollars coming from the airline, remember? For their luggage screwup?"

"Right," she said. "We need to get you a nice pair of black slacks, too."

"Black pants? Why?"

"Because you're going to wear them with one of my white blouses when you help me serve at Solange's exhibit opening."

Whiskey tango foxtrot?

I tried not to freak visibly. "Actually—" I started to say.

"Stop using that word," Mom snapped. "Just say what you want to say."

"Okay," I snapped back. "Here's the thing: I don't want to be your server in Madrid."

"We'll talk about it later," Mom said firmly.

Oh, great. This means it's a done deal in her darkened brain. I'm going to be forced to serve food at Solange's stupid event in Madrid. Which means the only way I'll be able to meet Webb will be at the damn event. And then he'll see me in a dorky waitress outfit. This is NOT going to happen.

I had to switch gears quickly. I had to e-mail Webb and tell him this meeting thing wasn't going to work out after all.

While Mom was on the ground level of Galeries Lafayette, shopping for makeup, I snuck up to the electronics department on the fourth floor and found a demo laptop with an Internet connection. I honestly planned to log on to my e-mail account and send Webb a message, suggesting we try to meet in St. Louis sometime in May. I was going to use "Meet Me in St. Louis?" as the subject line.

I wasn't prepared for the e-mail I found waiting for me.

Fr: Webbn@com
To: CocoChi@com
Subject: Re: About your bag

My answer:
(h) fall madly in love.
Your move, Blouse Girl.

CHAPTER 19

Andrew

J had enough on my mind. I didn't need to worry about Webb, too.

But after waiting two and a half hours for him, I gave up and walked back to the hotel. There I found my son, alone, in the business center, hypnotized by a computer screen. A half-eaten sandwich sat next to him on a grease-stained napkin.

I didn't know whether to be relieved or angry. We were in Europe, for God's sake. He should've been at the Prado, soaking up art. He should've been at the Plaza Mayor, sneaking a beer. Or he should've been at the Crystal Palace with *me*, where I goddamn *told* him to be.

But if he was going to disobey me, I would've preferred that he do so in at least an interesting way, rather than playing mind-numbing computer games or whatever the hell he was doing. Why wasn't he admiring beautiful young women and falling in love like I did at his age?

Before I became a first-class ass.

I had to stop thinking about that stupid note.

I tried to focus instead on Webb. Ever since he became a teenager, my son had done everything he could *not* to spend time with me. That was okay. That part I understood. But if he didn't want to be with me, why couldn't he be with someone or something more interesting than a computer? Why must the competition for my son's attention be something so dull and banal? I was prepared to tell him exactly that when I opened the door to the business center.

"Hey, Dad," Webb said. "What's up?"

The feral smell of dirty socks mixed with chorizo sausage and teenage boy hit me like a club.

"Jesus Christ, Webb," I said, covering my mouth and nose with both hands. "We've got to get you some clean clothes. *Now.*"

CHAPTER 20

Daisy

*I*t was worth five hundred dollars to make Coco think the airline was buying her such lovely things. Somehow, it made shopping more enjoyable for her.

But I confess a part of me—the part of me I don't like very much—thought: *Open your eyes, Coco! I'm the one paying for all this. There's no Santa Claus and no five-hundred-dollar check from the airline!*

But of course I couldn't say that, just like I couldn't stop myself from buying a pair of nice black pants for her when she wasn't looking. Solange wouldn't want Coco in jeans for the exhibit opening. And they were beautiful slacks. Coco could wear them for years. Somewhere down the line she'd thank me for buying them for her.

Or would she? Would I ever get credit for the ten zillion

little things I'd done for her that she didn't realize I was doing? Or was parenting as thankless as it seemed?

Of course it was.

It didn't matter. We were in Paris and having a good time—*finally*. I was relieved that she was being flexible enough (not her usual strong suit) to agree to go to Madrid. I really couldn't let Solange down. She'd been so generous over the years about letting me stay in her apartment. And how hard could it be to whip up hors d'oeuvres to satisfy a few hundred art patrons?

The only problem was trying to decide what people might want. Oh yeah, *that*. Not my strong suit.

I asked Coco over a late lunch what she thought people wanted. We were eating *moules frites* at a café near Solange's apartment. I'd always had a weakness for the Parisian combination of steamed mussels served in a heavy enamel pot with a side of salty french fries and a beer.

"What do people *want*?" Coco repeated, prying a mussel from its black shell. "Well, you really can't talk about *wants* until you talk about *needs*. And for that, you have to start with Abraham Maslow and his hierarchy of needs."

"Hmmm," I said. "Remind me what that is again?"

I had meant what people might want to *eat* at the exhibit opening, but I was happy to take the conversational detour. At home, Coco and I could go weeks without really talking. It was refreshing to hear what was on her mind.

"Well, I had the class last year," Coco said by way of disclaimer. "So I'm not sure if this is exactly right. But this guy, Abraham Maslow, had a theory about human needs."

Coco was interested in psychology. Like all girls her age, she was drawn to the study of psychoses and neuroses. She enjoyed memorizing the warning signs of each disorder and determining whether any of them was attractive enough to suit her or unattractive enough to describe her mother.

"He said," Coco continued, "that our needs are like a pyramid that builds upon itself. First, you have to satisfy basic needs, like food, water, air, sleep. Then you move up to the need for security. And then you have social needs, which are like family and love and stuff. And then esteem needs. And then the highest need is what he called the self-actualizing need, which is where people have the need to fulfill their potential. Or whatever."

I stopped listening when she got to the need for family and love. I was remembering a professor I'd had in college. He was a Jesuit priest. I wished I could remember his name. He said Mass at ten o'clock on Sunday nights at a tiny stone chapel in the middle of that cold Wisconsin campus.

In his homilies, this old Jesuit always talked about desire, and how we were connected by our desires. He said the most basic human desire was the desire to be desired by one you desire. I remembered how the priest almost cried when he talked about it.

God, were we all so lonely? I sipped a second beer. I didn't even like beer, but it traditionally came with *moules frites,* and I had appropriated for myself the beer that arrived with Coco's meal.

Coco was still talking. "So this Maslow guy said you could

tell who was self-actualized—meaning, who was at the top of the needs pyramid—because they were the people who were spontaneous and unconventional and really into peak experiences."

"What's a peak experience again?"

"*Mo-oooom,*" Coco said, exasperated by my ignorance. "You know, like when you have just a supergreat time, and it makes you feel really happy and inspired and totally, like, transformed. Like this." She leaned across the table so close that our faces were almost touching. "This is totally a peak experience."

I felt like reaching over and covering her with kisses. She seemed so happy. And hopeful. This was *my* daughter. I loved that she had the capacity to feel such joy.

"And Madrid will be fun, too, right?" I added cautiously, knowing that I was pushing my luck. "Won't it be fun to see Solange?"

"Yeah," she said softly. Then she took a deep, theatrical breath. "But I actually have to tell you something."

Never mind the "actually." I was too focused on what might follow. Oh, God. Was this why she was so moody? She wasn't even sexually active. (*Was she?*) She couldn't possibly be pregnant. (*Could she?*)

"It's really important," she said.

I *knew* I didn't like that Jack kid she was spending time with over winter break. Her gay guy friends were so much nicer, smarter, and more mature than her straight guy friends. Or did I think that only because I considered them safer?

"What is it, honey?" I asked, holding her hand. I did so

more to steady myself than her. My breathing was becoming increasingly shallow as I searched my brain, trying to think who it could be. *I'll kill him. Whoever it is, I will kill him with my bare hands.*

Coco sighed deeply. "I can't help you out on that serving thing in Madrid."

I was equal parts relieved and infuriated. "Why not?"

"Because I look like a *dork* in black pants and a white blouse," she stated unequivocally.

"Coco, don't be ridiculous."

"Mother, please! Don't make me do it. You *can't* make me do this. It's totally bad for my self-esteem."

Damn her and her self-esteem! Of course it'd be easier for me to let her off the hook. But didn't she owe me a few hours of light labor for bringing her to Paris? And what about Solange? After all the thoughtful gifts she'd sent Coco over the years—cashmere sweaters, signed museum prints, the Harry Potter books. First editions! Only to be rewarded now by this relentless self-absorbed brooding and vain preening? This boorish self-involvement?

"Coco, I'm sorry. But I really *do* need your help. And so does Solange."

She slouched resentfully and stared at her plate. Her eyes were moist with tears. "You're *trying* to ruin my life, aren't you? You want everyone to be alone and unhappy. Just like you."

Be nice to me, I was tempted to say. *I am all you have.*

Sure, she had grandparents—my parents—who spoiled her rotten. But they wouldn't be around forever. And I was an only child, so there were no aunts or uncles. Or cousins.

Maybe I should've adopted a child so Coco would have someone to lean on or collapse against when life turned cruel. But I didn't. So she was stuck with me. Me! Didn't she get that? *I'm all you have.* Me and my wonderful friends like Solange. But mostly me. *And you treat me like this?*

I attempted to remain civil. "What does my being single have to do with anything?"

"It's *all* related, Mom," she said, slamming her fork on the table. "The universe is *all* one. You know I'm *trying* to be a Buddhist!"

Oh, God. I finished Coco's beer in one gulp.

CHAPTER 21

Webb

I could tell Dad was thoroughly fed up with me.

"This is our second day in Madrid," he said. "And this is the first you've been out of the hotel?"

We were at El Corte Inglés, which is Madrid's equivalent of Macy's. Dad was watching me dig through a pile of jeans on a table in the men's department. I was trying to find something that didn't have decorative stitching on the back pockets. *What was with these Spanish guys and their disco jeans?*

"Look, Webb," he said. "Maybe you didn't want to come on this trip. Maybe you would've rather stayed home with your friends. But you're here now, and I wish you'd make the most of it."

"Okay," I said, resigning myself to the fact that I wasn't going to be able to find a pair of plain Levi's. Would it be better to meet Coco wearing the same jeans I'd been in since we left St. Louis or these stupid rhinestone cowboy jeans?

"I can't do the job I was brought here to do *and* worry about you," Dad continued. "All I ask for is just a little courtesy."

"Sorry," I said.

Maybe I could wash the jeans I was wearing in the hotel sink and dry them with a hair dryer. That'd be better than these blingy jeans. I turned my attention to shirts. At least they were normal. I grabbed two plain blue T-shirts that looked my size.

"If you weren't going to come to the exhibit space this morning," Dad was saying, "you could've called and let me know."

"Sorry," I repeated.

This would be so much easier if I could just tell him the reason I was at the hotel: that I was planning to meet a girl I really liked. But I couldn't tell him. He'd make way too big a deal of it.

"I know you're sorry," Dad said. "But . . ." He was staring at the clothes I held in my hands. "You're going to need something nicer than that for the opening."

The museum exhibit opening. Damn. I forgot. How was I going to get out of that?

"Look, Webb," he continued. "Tomorrow night's going to be crazy. There are going to be a lot of people at the opening: artists, patrons, museum board members, and so forth. I have to talk to them and be available for questions or problems. I can't be worrying about where you are and what you're doing."

"Right," I said. Then it occurred to me. "Want me to just text you every couple hours? So you know I'm okay?"

His face looked like a big question mark. "I thought you forgot your cell phone at school."

"I did. But I can send you an e-mail from anywhere. There are Internet connections all over the place. At the hotel, in cafés, probably even at the exhibit."

"Of course," Dad said, smiling for the first time in hours. "It's a digital show. I'm sure there'll be places for you to get online. Good thinking, Webb."

I felt like high-fiving Dad for agreeing to this plan, which completely freed me up to blow off the thing at the museum.

He wandered over to a rack of suits. Minutes later he returned, holding a navy blue Polo blazer in my size.

"Sorry," I said, shaking my head. "Ain't gonna happen."

"Webb, you can't wear a T-shirt to opening night," he said. "Wear this jacket with a white dress shirt and jeans."

"I don't have a white shirt," I said. "It was in my bag."

"We'll get you a new shirt," Dad said. "What shoes do you have?"

"Just my Chucks," I said, gesturing to my feet.

"I'd prefer leather," Dad answered, pulling his chin like a professor. "But it is a postmodern show. I guess those will be okay."

Fine. Whatever. I'll get whatever he wants me to get. I can change in a bathroom if I need to.

Dad had to get back to work on the exhibit space.

"Let's meet at the hotel at seven for dinner," Dad said, putting me in a cab. "We'll get some paella. You like that, remember?"

I did remember. But of course all I could think about was checking my e-mail. I was dying to know how Coco had responded to my suggestion. Why the hell *not* fall in love?

Of course it was easy to be bold online. But seriously, I was seventeen years old. I was in Europe, for God's sake. Shouldn't I be falling in love?

When I made it back to the hotel, I dumped the Corte Inglés bags on the floor in the business center and logged on to my e-mail account. One new message.

Fr: CocoChi@com
To: Webbn@com
Subject: What a tangled Webb …

Spidey, you're adorable. And falling in love sounds like fun. Really! (And from the full disclosure department: I've never done it before. Have you?) But ugh and merde! I'm afraid this isn't going to work. My mom is being a total Blackhawk. As in helicopter mama gone apeshit. I don't think I'm going to be able to break away from her while we're in Madrid. I am SO SORRY about this!!! It is no reflection on you, I promise. Please write back so I know you're not mad. I'm totally upset about this. We should've been the stuff movies are made of, y'know?

Coco

CHAPTER 22

Coco

I don't know if it was jet lag or the mussels we had for lunch or the stress of meeting—or not meeting—Webb. Whatever the reason, I wasn't hungry for dinner that night. Neither was Mom. But I needed to check my e-mail.

"Actually, something sweet sounds good," I told Mom. We were walking back to the apartment from the Metro stop. "Can I pick up some treats for us at the patisserie across the street from Solange's place?"

"Good idea," Mom said. "Get me something lemony. I've gotta call Solange."

"Cool," I said. "I'll meet you in the apartment in a few minutes."

After I saw her put her key in the front door to Solange's building, I ducked into the Internet café to see if Webb had responded. He had.

Fr: Webbn@com
To: CocoChi@com
Subject: Re: What a tangled Webb . . .

    Not mad, just disappointed. Mr. Hitchcock had such
high hopes for us.
    (And no, I've never done it before, either.)

Love,
Webb

Love? I stared at the word. Love. What a sweet boy. Okay,
I *had* to make this work.

Fr: CocoChi@com
To: Webbn@com
Subject: Re: Re: What a tangled Webb . . .

    I know. I'm disappointed, too!
Love,
Coco

I studied my message before sending it. Coming from me,
"Love" seemed forced. I deleted the word. But then that looked
cold. So I deleted my name, too, and pressed SEND.
His response arrived seconds later.

Fr: Webbn@com
To: CocoChi@com
Subject: Re: Re: Re: What a tangled Webb . . .

Can I suggest an alternative? (Tell me now if I'm
wasting my time.)

Fr: CocoChi@com
To: Webbn@com
Subject: Re: Re: Re: Re: What a tangled Webb . . .

No! I mean, yes! Suggest away! I really DO want to
meet you.

Fr: Webbn@com
To: CocoChi@com
Subject: Re: Re: Re: Re: Re: What a tangled Webb . . .

Okay, here goes. What if instead of meeting in
Madrid, we met in Paris? Could you convince your *madre*
that you've got some kinda bug—I don't know, maybe

like spontaneous leprosy or something—and you're too
sick to fly to Madrid tmw? If so, I could take a morning
train up to Paris and meet you there tmw pm. Without
the weirdness of parents. I'd return before your mom gets
back—or my dad notices I'm gone. Brilliant or stupid?
You tell me.

Fr: CocoChi@com
To: Webbn@com
Subject: Re: Re: Re: Re: Re: Re: What a tangled Webb...

   OMG. You're brilliant! Do trains run between Paris and
Madrid?

Fr: Webbn@com
To: CocoChi@com
Subject: Re: Re: Re: Re: Re: Re: Re: What a tangled Webb...

   Looking at the online sked now. Leave here tmw morn
at 8:45. Arrive in Paris at 10:41 pm. Depart Paris the
next morn at 7:10. Arrive Madrid 7:42 pm.

Fr: CocoChi@com
To: Webbn@com
Subject: Re: Re: Re: Re: Re: Re: Re: Re: What a tangled Webb ...

   OMGx2. Let's do it!!!

Fr: Webbn@com
To: CocoChi@com
Subject: Re: Re: Re: Re: Re: Re: Re: Re: Re: What a
tangled Webb ...

   Serious?

Fr: CocoChi@com
To: Webbn@com
Subject: Re: Re: Re: Re: Re: Re: Re: Re: Re: Re: What a tangled
Webb ...

   100%. Can you check your e-mail tomorrow morning
before you leave? Just to make sure I can weasel out of
going to Madrid? Not certain I can pull this off. but I'm
going to TRY TRY TRY! The good thing is. I had a really

high fever once when Mom/I were flying to L.A.. and I passed out cold as soon as we landed at LAX. It ended up being nothing. but my mother toooottallly freaked. So this might just work!

Fr: Webbn@com
To: CocoChi@com
Subject: Re: Re: Re: Re: Re: Re: Re: Re: Re: Re: Re: What a tangled Webb . . .

Try, Blousey. That's all I can ask. Mr. Hitchcock is rooting for us.

By the time I got back to the apartment, I was a complete wreck. Luckily Mom was still on the phone. When she hung up, she stared at me: "Where's dessert?"

"Oh," I said. "I forgot."

"Honey, what's wrong with you? You're white as a sheet."

I flopped facedown on the futon. "My stomach feels funny." And I was only half lying.

CHAPTER 23

Andrew

I spent the rest of the day putting out fires at the exhibition space.

Someone—a disgruntled laborer was my guess—had apparently flushed wet cement down the toilets in the women's restroom. I had to find an industrial plumber to clear the lines. Meanwhile, an electrician was working on the shades, which were cooperating but only intermittently. It would all get resolved by the time the exhibition opened the following evening.

My bigger concern was the show itself. Was art getting worse, or was I getting more jaded? Because this show, with all its monitors and high-tech digital effects, left me cold.

If these artists were trying to convince me that the pursuit of love in the postdigital age was more exciting, more mysterious, more . . . well, *everything* love should be, they'd failed. None of the exhibits passed the Jimmy Webb test, which was the standard by which I judged all works of art.

The test consisted of comparing the work in question with the song "Wichita Lineman," where the tension between what you understood and what you didn't was just the right mix to pull you in deeper. Art has to ask questions and make you care. Nothing I saw elicited even the slightest emotional response. But maybe that was the point. Maybe love was impossible in the postdigital age. Maybe passion was passé.

Or maybe I was just too old to understand it—or worse yet, to experience it. When was the last time I'd been with a woman who moved me half as much as a Jimmy Webb song? Moira in grad school? Blythe during my internship in New York? Frances, later, in Vancouver? They all eventually tired of my inability to fully connect, and who could blame them? And then when Laura got pregnant with Webb, that changed everything.

Never mind the past. I had to focus on the show.

After I finally had the electronic shades working to my satisfaction, I returned to the hotel to put on a clean shirt for dinner. Webb was in the room, watching soccer on TV.

"Hungry for paella?" I asked while buttoning my shirt.

"Uh-huh," he answered.

"So how'd you spend your afternoon?" I asked, hoping to be surprised.

"Yeah, uh-huh," he said. His eyes didn't move from the TV.

"What'd you do this afternoon?"

"Uh, nothing really. But I want to do some stuff tomorrow. Hey, Dad, can I have some euros?"

I gave him a stack of bills. At least he'd put on the new clothes.

We walked from the hotel over to Plaza de Santa Ana, a photogenic old square filled with street musicians and tapas bars. I chose a restaurant with a nice crowd of locals.

"I'm going to have wine with dinner," I said as Webb and I seated ourselves at a small table near the back. "You can have a glass, if you'd like. It's legal here."

"Enh, pass," he said. "I'll just have a Coke."

As we waited for our paella, I couldn't help staring at Webb. For years I'd done my best to make sure he was cautious, careful, not too much of a risk taker. I wanted to help him learn to make smart choices, unlike his mother.

But maybe I'd gone too far. Maybe I'd created a young man who was a coward—or worse yet, a dullard.

"What's the favorite thing you've seen so far on this trip?" I asked.

He didn't answer.

"Webb," I said. "What's the best thing you've done so far in Madrid?"

He still didn't respond. He had a faraway look in his eyes. Somehow he wasn't hearing the impatience in my voice.

"Webb, dammit, I'm talking to you!"

"Sorry," he said. "I was thinking about something else."

Thinking seemed like a pretty generous word for it, I thought as I poured a second glass of wine from the carafe. With the alcohol came a depressing thought: *Who am I to call anyone a bore? I'm a first-class ass.*

That stupid note was like a rock in my shoe. *So what* if I

had slipped an admiring note in a woman's bag? Was it such a goddamn crime? Part of me knew it wasn't. But the other, more honest part of me wondered if it wasn't the beginning of the end. Because it wasn't just the note-in-the-bag debacle. There was also the fact that I clearly didn't understand or appreciate the *Love in the Postdigital Age* exhibit. Maybe I was too old for this stuff. Maybe I'd lost my eye for modern art. Would I soon start defending the work of Thomas Kinkade and collecting keepsakes from the Franklin Mint? Did the fact that I'd so misjudged the appropriateness of a romantic gesture mean I'd lost my compass in that realm, too? Would I start pinching women's asses in elevators—or frequenting Hooters? Was I turning into a pig?

"Dad, don't you think?" Webb was asking me.

"What?" I said.

"Just . . . everything," he said, laughing and making a sweeping gesture with his hand. "I like everything here. Don't you?"

"Yeah," I said.

With the possible exception of myself.

CHAPTER 24

Daisy

P oor Coco.

Normally I would've blamed the mussels. But I'd had them, too, along with two beers, and felt fine.

Before she curled up on the futon to sleep, Coco had complained that her head was throbbing. Shortly before midnight, I heard her in the bathroom, rummaging through Solange's medicine cabinet. I got up to check on her.

"What do you need, honey?" I asked.

"Aspirin. Tylenol. Anything," she said, holding her head.

Her skin was chalk white, but she didn't feel feverish. I got some nighttime formula Excedrin from my bag and gave her two capsules. "Do you want a wet washcloth for your head?"

"No," she whimpered.

"Go back to sleep. You'll feel better in the morning."

She looked at me with her big, kitten-in-a-basket eyes. "Mom, I don't think I can go to Madrid with you."

"Oh, Coco. We have to do this. I'm sorry. I really am, but—"

"Mom, I *can't*," she cried, her voice breaking into a kind of wail. "I will seriously throw up or pass out or *something* if I have to get on a plane."

My mind became a murky blur of dark images. I couldn't let Solange down. I just couldn't. But how could I drag Coco to Madrid if she really felt this bad? I remembered the time at LAX when I thought she'd died.

Oh, God. This is what I get for wanting to throttle my daughter earlier in the day. This is my punishment for being a terrible mother.

"Do you think you need to see a doctor?" I asked.

"No," Coco said, gulping for air. "It's just like . . . a bug or something. Can't you go without me?"

"I can't leave you here alone."

"Why not?"

"Because I *can't*," I said, picking up the phone and dialing Solange's number.

She answered on the first ring. Of course Solange was awake at this late hour.

"I hate to do this to you," I said after explaining the situation. "But I knew you'd understand."

"I do understand," Solange replied. "But, Daisy, I need you here. Would Coco be more comfortable on a train?"

I asked. Coco buried her head and started crying.

"I'm afraid she *really* doesn't feel well," I said.

Solange asked to talk to Coco. I could hear only my daughter's end of the conversation.

"Hi . . . Thanks . . . I know . . . No, it's nothing like that. It's just . . . I feel crummy. I'm sure it's nothing . . . Of course I wouldn't mind. I know! College, right? I'm going to be on my own in four months anyway."

Of course she'd already begun the countdown for when she was leaving me. It's okay. Perfectly normal, in fact. Don't take it personally.

"Uh-huh," Coco was now saying. "Yeah, okay. Thanks. I will. Bye."

She handed the phone back to me.

"The problem is solved," Solange reported. "Coco will stay in bed and get better. You will call Coco from Madrid every four hours. She has music, DVDs, TV, and a refrigerator full of food."

"But—" I objected.

"You will leave Paris tomorrow morning and be back the next morning," Solange reminded me.

"That's a whole day," I said.

"D'accord," Solange said. "And Coco will be in *bed*. If she starts to feel worse, I will have my doctor go and look at her."

"Doctors make house calls in Paris?" I asked.

Coco lifted her head. "Of course they do, Mom. Didn't I tell you to see *Sicko*?"

Her superior tone coupled with her ability to keep a running tally of my flaws convinced me that she was already on the road to recovery.

"Daisy, you have the best daughter in the universe," Solange was saying. "You can trust her to stay in my apartment for twenty-some hours, for God's sake."

"D'accord," I said. "I *do* have a great kid."

Coco looked at me and smiled.

So I agreed to keep my commitment to Solange. And part of me—that secret part I really and truly don't like very much—was grateful to have an excuse to spend some time on my own away from my perfect kid, whose only fault was that, at times, she reminded me exactly of me.

Day 3: Tuesday

To buy in Madrid

- butter
- lemon
- sugar
- flour
- chocolate
- vanilla

IBERIA LINEAS AEREAS
(Boarding Pass)

SPRINKLE

IBERIA

TARJETA DE EMBARQUE (Boarding Pass)

DAISY M. SPRINKLE

PARIS (ORY)

MADRID (MAD)

IBERIA LINEAS AEREAS

IB 3403   K 19APR 10AM

D62   9:50   21E

113

21E
113

Nombre de Pasajero: Adulto Nino
WEBB G. NELSON   ONE   NIL

           Fecha   Numero
           19.04   13303   1226○5568S30

From
MADRID   08:45   Ticket Type
To
PARIS   22.41   DAY RETURN

CHAPTER 25

Webb

$\mathcal{I}$ didn't sleep much that night. Could've been the paella, but more likely I was stressing about meeting Coco.

Somewhere around 2:00 A.M., when I was sure Dad was zonked, I got out of bed and pulled on my jeans and a shirt. I grabbed a room key and went downstairs to the business center to check e-mail.

Nothing from Coco, so I read some of the other messages I'd been ignoring the last few days. They were all from friends at school.

Fr: Archboy@com
To: Webbn@com
Subject: Wassup???

hey wassup someone said yr in costa ricka or russhia or s/ware izzat right well b cool and stay safe you missed a bitchin party last pm at gavin's house no parents + lotsa beer + laaaadies

Fr: Methatswho@com
To: Webbn@com
Subject: w/r r u?
Attached: You gottta hear this!

hey webbmaster. didnt c u @ G's party and yr not r/trnin my t/msgs or calls u ok? g's party was awsumest of the year open this file. u wont bleeve yr ears

I clicked on the attachment and was treated to the sound of farts performing the opening bars of Beethoven's Fifth Symphony.

I hit CANCEL and closed the file. I decided to reread Coco's messages instead.

It wasn't my imagination. She *was* different. Unlike my friends, she sounded alive. Awake. She was funny, which meant she was also smart. And she was polite, which meant she was also nice. Best of all, she seemed to like me. Me! ME! ME!!! Which, I admit, made me like *her* even more.

I decided to reread the messages I'd sent her. Hell, I didn't sound half bad myself. But it was easy to sound good in e-mail, especially if you were operating under the assumption that the person you were writing to liked you.

Was *that* how it worked? You just find someone and agree

to like each other—and then take it from there? Jesus H. Christ. This was so much more fun than wandering around like a pack of wolves with my dumbass guy friends who lived in the hopes of hooking up with a pack of willing she-wolves— preferably she-wolves with big boobs. It wasn't even fun. It was boring and depressing.

This was fun. Coco was fun.

Thinking about her made me feel strangely energized, so I went for a walk. It was pitch-dark, but the city was still wide awake. Cabs raced past the hotel. A couple kissed on the hotel steps, the girl folded into the guy's arms.

How did people learn to do these things? And why weren't there classes at school for stuff like this—the stuff kids really *wanted* to learn? Kissing seemed so natural for this couple. I wanted to watch them more closely but, Christ, I didn't want to stare. So I kept walking.

I crossed the street to a narrow, tree-lined park that ran the length of Paseo del Prado. A group of sketchy-looking guys had a card table set up with stuff on it. They yelled something to me in Spanish, which I didn't catch. Probably for the best. Then they were waving something at me. One of the guys had matches. Were they selling drugs? The matches guy was lighting something.

Oh, sparklers. They were selling sparklers!

I hadn't thought about sparklers in forever. My dad used to put sparklers on my birthday cake every year. We also lit them on New Year's Eve. Dad had home movies of me running around in my Indiana Jones pajamas at midnight, holding sparklers over my head and squealing.

Matches Guy was saying something to me. "Para tí, cinco euros." He was waving a handful of five sparklers at me.

Five sparklers for five euros? That seemed reasonable. I reached in my pocket and pulled out a five-euro bill. Matches Guy took the money and handed me four sparklers.

"Uno más," I said, pretty sure that was Spanish for *one more*.

They laughed and pretended not to understand me—or the fact that I knew I'd just been rooked one sparkler.

I should've moved on. I should've known better than to try to be a tough guy with them. Judging from their business hours and retail space, they were marginal characters with thuggish leanings. But I wanted my fifth sparkler, dammit.

"Five for five," I said. "Cinco por cinco."

They suddenly stopped laughing.

"¿Qué dijó?" Matches Guy asked.

"Cinco por cinco," I said again.

The guys looked at one another and took off running, leaving their card table and sparklers behind.

I helped myself to a sparkler—I *had* paid for it, after all— and kept walking.

Sparklers. This was perfect. I'd take them to Paris and give them to Coco when I met her at the train station.

Or maybe I'd keep them with me and light one after we kissed for the first time. And if there was other stuff to follow, well, I'd light a sparkler to commemorate that. I wouldn't have to tell her it was my first time. Or maybe I would. She sounded like a girl who'd be cool with that. I'd just have to play it by ear.

I walked back to the hotel and took the stairs up to our fourth-floor room. I opened the door quietly, careful not to wake Dad. He was out cold. After slipping the sparklers inside my (or, really Coco's) duffel bag, I lay in bed wide awake until the sun came up. I was equal parts exhausted and excited.

This is what New Year's Eve used to feel like, I thought, impatient as an eight-year-old boy for the day to begin.

CHAPTER 26

Coco

𝒥 thought Mom would *never* leave.

And I really *did* feel crummy that the very last thing I'd said to her, after she asked for the five-hundredth time if I was okay with her leaving was: *Mother, I cannot get better with you hovering over me like this!*

Honestly, I wanted to strangle myself when I said stuff like that to her. But it was almost like I couldn't help it. My bratty, eight-year-old self was always more verbal than my trying-to-be-nice eighteen-year-old self. I knew I was überstressing about meeting Webb and taking it out on Mom. But of course I couldn't tell *her* that.

When she was finally gone, I threw on some clothes and ran down to the Internet place. My fingers flew across the keyboard.

Fr: CocoChi@com
To: Webbn@com
Subject: Strangers on a Train Platform

Spidey!

My mom just left. Believe it or not, I really DID get sick,
but I'm feeling much better now. Think I was just nervous.
(You too?) Anyway, I'll meet you tonight. Just tell me which
station and I'll be there, OK?
Blouse Girl

P.S. I'll wear an article of your clothing for easy
identification.

I waited. Was it possible he'd given up on me? Or maybe
he'd chickened out. Before I could consider other possibilities,
I had a new message.

Fr: Webbn@com
To: CocoChi@com
Subject: Re: Strangers on a Train Platform

Thanks for coming up with a title for our little scheme.
And please don't worry yourself sick. I'm the most
harmless guy you (don't) know.

Leaving here pronto. I'll bring your bag. I like the idea
of you wearing something of mine. I'll wear something
of yours, too. We'll switch clothes in some dramatic and
Hitchcockian way.

Station = Gare de Lyon. See you there at 10:41 pm.

Love,
Spidey

Oh my God. There it was again: *Love.*

Suddenly I felt sick to my stomach—again. *Switch clothes
in some dramatic and Hitchcockian way?* Was he suggesting we
strip each other like in a creepy porn flick?

I read the message again. *Our little scheme?* Did he think
we were going to have sex?

Then I quickly reread all of his messages, searching for
clues. They were everywhere.

*(h) fall madly in love . . . I haven't done it, either. But I'm
ready . . . Try, Blousey. That's all I can ask. Mr. Hitchcock is
rooting for us.*

Shit. He definitely wanted to have sex.

Okay, granted, having sex was on my to-do list before I left
for college. I definitely did not want to be the only girl in the
freshman class at Washington University who *hadn't* done it.
And maybe the first time would be easier with someone you
never had to see again. Maybe this was perfect!

Okay, it was perfect. So why was I completely freaked?

Because I didn't even know this guy. What was I thinking? Why were we moving so fast? And what about birth control? Someone was going to have to bring that up. I hoped it didn't have to be me. I mean, I *could*. And I would if I absolutely *had* to. My mother had been harping on the importance of safe sex since I was six years old. But she'd neglected to tell me the most important part: *Who brings the condoms—the girl or the guy?*

When I got back to the apartment, I plugged in the electric kettle for tea. While the water was heating up, I flipped through my Paris guidebooks in a frenzy. I knew I'd seen something in one of the books about buying condoms in Paris. Where was it? Shit! *Where the hell was it?!*

Oh, here: *The only place to buy condoms in Paris is at a pharmacy.*

Webb's train wasn't scheduled to arrive until late. *Would pharmacies still be open then? Should I go out and buy some condoms now—just in case?*

Oh, God. I was starting to work myself up into a full-blown panic attack. If I got hives on top of this, I'd kill myself.

I turned off the teakettle. Then I took all of Webb's clothes out of his bag and examined them, article by article, like a criminal psychologist. Unmatched tube socks. (Was he careless or carefree?) Three Speed Stick deodorant stubs. (Manly and sweaty or OCD issues?) Rumpled jeans and shirts. (Typical guy or a red herring?) His dog-eared copy of *Walden*. (At least he's a reader. But Thoreau? Bit of a slacker.) Plain boxer shorts with the little flap in the front. (Okay, he's a boy. So he has a . . .)

I ran back to the Internet place so I could reread all of

Webb's e-mails slowly, from beginning to end. With each message I read, I breathed a little more easily. *Need I tell you what my nickname was in elementary school? Charlotte.*

With a childhood nickname like Charlotte, he couldn't be a sex maniac. In fact, he sounded really nice. And funny. And smart. A triple threat, as my friends and I called the nice/funny/smart combo platter. And his plaid boxer shorts were cute.

As I walked back to the apartment for the second time that morning, my mind spun like a kaleidoscope with a dizzying combination of thoughts: *I can't believe I'm going to have sex tonight!!!!!!!!!!!!! Will it hurt? Will we laugh? Would I cry? Would he secretly think I was fat? Or ugly? Or beautiful? What would I say? Would he be nervous, too? Should I compliment his . . . Hitchcock?*

Then a terrible idea occurred to me: *What if Webb was into tantric sex, that hippie style of sex that lasts all night?*

Ugh. I just wanted to do it and get it *over* with.

My first real date and my first sexual experience. I'd kill two birds with one stone. *Or wait, that's rude to birds.*

Feed two birds with one meal. *That* was it.

I made a cup of tea and then left the apartment in search of a pharmacy.

CHAPTER 27

Andrew

I woke up to the sound of singing. I cursed, thinking the noise was coming from the room next door. Then I glanced at Webb's bed: empty.

Minutes later, Webb emerged from the bathroom. He was freshly showered and wearing one of the plush terry-cloth robes provided by the hotel. I noted the rare appearance of comb marks through his wet hair.

"You're up early," I said. Then I remembered something. "Webb, were you awake in the middle of the night?"

"Uh-huh," he answered. "I couldn't sleep. So I went downstairs to check e-mail."

"Jesus Christ, Webb. Why didn't you just use my BlackBerry? You can get to your Facebook account or e-mail on it."

"No can do," Webb said, smiling slyly. "Privacy."

"Right." And with that I heard my BlackBerry buzz. Eight

new messages—all from Solange. And it wasn't even seven o'clock.

I realized I probably wouldn't have time to return to the hotel and change before the gala, so I hung a jacket, shirt, and tie on a hanger. I felt tired just thinking of all the things that had to be done in the next twelve and a half hours.

"You're going to wear your new jacket tonight, right?" I asked Webb.

"Yep," he said with a faint note of excitement in his voice. I was pleased he liked the jacket.

"And you're going to do a better job keeping in touch with me today, right?"

"Correct," he answered.

"Great. I've gotta get moving. And tomorrow morning, I plan on sleeping in. So no singing in the shower, please."

"Won't happen," Webb said in a happy voice.

He was certainly in a good mood. His color even seemed better. He looked less pale. His cheeks were almost rosy. Then it hit me like a brick to the forehead. It was obvious what Webb's problem had been the past two days, and why he was suddenly so light on his feet.

He'd been constipated.

I mentally kicked myself for not picking up on the clues earlier. *What kind of unobservant parent was I?*

CHAPTER 28

Daisy

As soon as I left for the airport, I regretted it.

What if it wasn't a stomach bug? What if it was food poisoning? What if she became dangerously dehydrated? People died from that.

And leaving her alone in a foreign country? *What kind of mother was I?*

Then again, maybe Solange was right. Coco was eighteen. She'd be on her own in the fall at college. I'd left her with a pile of euros, a list of phone numbers, tea, juice, plenty of food.

And, yes, she *was* the world's most responsible kid. I'd never had to worry about her—not her grades, not friends, not drugs, not drinking. If anything, she was *too* cautious. My financial planner told me this was common in women, especially those of us with deep streaks of perfectionism. We had to get better at taking risks, he said, and we had to encourage our daughters to do the same.

But leaving her alone—in Paris? What was I *thinking*? And how much of my willingness to leave her in bed for a day was a result of my desire to get the hell away from her? It was a terrible thing for a mother to admit, but there it was. My daughter could annoy me like no one else on earth. Her self-righteousness. Her piety. Her short temper and know-it-all attitude.

Of course I knew exactly where it came from: me. This was the hell of parenting—seeing all your worst qualities in someone else. And then there was the added frustration of being unable to change them in your child just as you were unable to change them in yourself.

At least Coco knew what she wanted. She wanted to study psychology at Washington University. And she would. She'd make a terrific psychologist. She had no qualms about dishing out advice, especially to me. *Mom, you've got to stop overtweezing your brows. Mom, you're so uptight. Mom, you have to start meditating!*

She was usually right. And she was certainly focused and driven. I just worried if she was happy. Of all the things I'd tried to teach her, that was the one area in which I'd failed. Sure, I'd taught her how to be a good student and get good grades, which translated into getting a good job as an adult. But there was more to life than work, wasn't there?

My mind flashed back to that annoying headline: "What Does Daisy Sprinkle Want?" Nancy thought I needed more therapy. I knew I needed a small vacation. Was it too horrible to admit that what I *really* wanted was a vacation from being a mother?

To say motherhood was a humbling profession didn't begin to describe it. And it wasn't just the lack of gratitude. That part I could handle. It wasn't even the god-awful macaroni and cheese and ridiculous *nuggets* children insisted they preferred to real food. It was the suffocation of it. The asphyxiation. That combined with the rejection. How ironic to find yourself at the wrong end of an unrequited love relationship with the very person you'd given birth to.

Was it too awful to admit I wanted a break from this?

Yes, it was awful. But honest, too.

As the plane took off, I pulled out my notebook and reviewed my shopping list: butter, lemon, sugar (white and powdered), baking soda, flour, chocolate, vanilla.

At first, Solange had been confused when I told her that I planned to serve predigital comfort food at her gala.

"What the hell are you talking about?" she said when she called at dawn to make sure I was still coming.

"Well, didn't you say this was an exhibition of artists who came of age in the postdigital world?" I asked.

"Yes," she said slowly.

"Okay, so that's the era when people stopped baking," I explained. "Everyone was too busy. Everyone was either at work, chained to a computer, or at home glued to a TV and video games."

"Just tell me what you are making," Solange said. She sounded nervous.

"Gooey butter cake," I said. "Texas sheet cake. Red velvet cake. Chocolate-chip cookies."

"Chocolate-*chimp* cookies!" cried Solange, her English

failing her by only one letter. "I have not thought about those in years. Not since you made them for me in Paris." Then she paused. "But Daisy, Europeans do not eat sweets like that. This I am sure."

"I know," I said. "So it will seem exotic to them and vaguely nostalgic, like a past they never knew. But it's the kind of food that makes you feel happy and sad, like when you want something, but can't quite name what it is."

"I am not sure what you mean," Solange said. "But I love you, and I have to go because the damn exhibit designer is making a million last-minute changes, and I feel like killing him. I will send a driver to pick you up at the airport at noon."

"Perfect," I said. "Wait! What about waiters? Servers? I was going to have Coco help me, but—"

"All taken care of," Solange interrupted. "The man I originally hired for this job, the baker whose father died, has a whole crew lined up. Handsome waiters with their own tuxes. It will be perfect! Kisses!"

CHAPTER 29

Webb

A fter I read Coco's message, I sprang into action.

First, I downloaded a free program that lets you send e-mail messages anytime you want. Then I wrote a bunch of vague e-mails to Dad to be sent every 2.68 hours.

Of course I felt guilty about missing Dad's big night. He'd been working on the design for this exhibit for more than a year. And I felt even guiltier lying to him. I knew my dad only wanted the best for me. But sometimes he didn't know what that was. I did. The best thing for me was to meet Coco Sprinkle in Paris.

I found the concierge in the lobby.

"You are looking for your father?" he asked. "He left the hotel ten minutes ago."

"Gracias, señor," I said. "But no, it's something else. No necesitamos, um, la ayuda con la casa en la sala 403 hoy día. Ni mañana."

"You do not need help with the house?" he asked.

"Housekeeping," I said. "Can you ask housekeeping not to visit room 403 today or tomorrow?"

He scribbled a note on a pad of paper. "It is done, señor."

"Gracias," I said.

I bolted back upstairs to the room, where I stuffed pillows in my bed and pulled the covers up over it, just like in a Disney movie. Then I grabbed Coco's bag and hung the PRIVADO/ PRIVACY sign on the door.

As I rode the Metro to the train station, I felt like I was in a dream. I could feel my life changing in a huge and fantastic way. I could already imagine myself telling the story to my dumbass friends. *You met a girl where?* they'd ask. *How? Are you shittin' me?*

I paid for my round-trip train ticket with the money Dad had given me. I hadn't realized how expensive it'd be. After buying the ticket, I had only twenty euros left when I boarded the train at eight thirty.

For the next thirteen-plus hours, I stared out the window at the passing towns and countryside. All those lives. All those untold stories and private dramas. There was something so beautiful and sad about it. I felt weirdly emotional, like I was running away from home, but also running to a new home. I ate a cheese sandwich on a baguette for lunch.

Hours later, I watched Spain turn into France. I had another cheese sandwich for dinner around six o'clock. After two sandwiches and a big bottle of water, I had only ten euros left. I tried to ignore my appetite.

As the sky darkened, I began to feel almost giddy with

excitement. The sound of the train seemed to be saying: *YESshelikesyou, YESshelikesyou, YESshelikesyou.* But even I realized the absurdity of that.

Okay, so she liked me a little bit, anyway. That much was obvious in her e-mails. But it was important to play it cool. Not to be an idiot. Suddenly the train started mocking me with the sounds of *JEEZyou'restupid, JEEZyou'restupid, JEEZyou'restupid.*

I remembered then that I'd forgotten to wash my jeans. The train answered my thought with *JEEZyoureekyoudumbshit, JEEZyoureekyoudumbshit, JEEZyoureekyoudumbshit.*

Finally at 10:40, the train pulled into the Paris station.

I was stiff from the long ride, and my left leg had fallen asleep. *Great. Now she's going to think I have cerebral palsy.* I stomped my foot hard and tried to get the blood circulating. I stepped off the train, holding Coco's bag in my right hand.

The other passengers seemed to be in a big hurry. I fell to the back of the pack as I walked down the platform. Somehow I wanted to delay the moment we met—to make the anticipation last as long as possible.

I knew her the second I saw her. She was standing under a clock. Her brown hair was pulled back in a ponytail. She was wearing my white shirt and carrying *Walden.*

She smiled at me.

I wanted to kiss her right then and there.

CHAPTER 30

Coco

$\mathcal{I}$ never would've guessed it was him. He looked so European!

He was wearing a crisp white shirt—possibly new—with perfectly decrepit Levi's and Chuck Taylor shoes. He even had a scarf around his neck, like all the French guys wear. It was only when he got closer and started to unwrap the scarf that I realized it was my peasant blouse.

"Blouse Girl?" Webb said, handing me my blouse.

"Yes, it's me," I said. "Hi!" I extended my hand to shake his, but he leaned in for a kiss.

"Aren't we supposed to do this?" he said, kissing both sides of my face in a funny, noncreepy way.

I laughed. "You're totally right."

"I think it's a great custom," he said.

"I know," I said. "It's like, *great,* right?"

He was smiling at me. "Yep, great."

"Totally great," I added. *Why was I repeating everything he said like an idiot?* "Are you exhausted? I can't believe you've been on a train all day."

"It wasn't bad," he said. "In fact it was kinda nice."

"Really?" I asked. *Why couldn't I think of one freakin' interesting thing to say? Why hadn't I prepared a funny little story to tell him?* "Hey, did you know the guillotine wasn't invented by Dr. Guillotin?"

"Seriously?" he said. "Who invented it?"

"Uh, I'm actually not sure. Dr. Guillotin just sorta, y'know, improved on the original design."

We stood there, staring at each other. Or at least I did. He seemed like Mr. Super Casual Cool while I apparently was working on my Girl Scout guillotine badge.

"What a cool train station," he finally said, looking around. "Why don't we have train stations like this at home?"

"I know," I said. "It's actually . . . great."

Ack! Mom was right about actually. It sounded stupid. I sounded stupid.

"Did you want to just hang here for while or . . ." he began.

"Oh, no," I said. "We can actual—, I mean, we should go back to the apartment. Are you hungry or tired? Do you want to get something to eat or just walk around the city?"

"Yes, yes, yes, and yes," he said. "And if I missed one, yes to that, too."

I laughed. "Well, you're certainly easy."

Oh God. Did I really just say that? But he was laughing. *Thank God.*

"I don't know about *easy*," he said, smiling. "But I am starving. And I'm dying to see Paris. C'mon. We've got eight hours till my train leaves."

CHAPTER 31

Andrew

I should've known. Because it's always the same.

The day before an exhibit opens, nothing—*absolutely nothing*—is right. But by show time, the art gods always smile down, and the opening reception is an unqualified success. Bad dress rehearsals make good opening nights and all that.

This show was no different. The exhibit area was filled with well-dressed Madrileños who were clearly enjoying the show, judging from their smiling faces, which were illuminated by the tiny blue twinkle lights I'd used to set off the space.

A successful opening always felt good, though I was too exhausted to enjoy this one. I looked for Webb among the crowd of cell-phone-carrying art patrons navigating through the *Spin the Cell Phone* installation. The pulsating techno beat was unbearable. I wandered off to the side with a piece of sweet, golden pastry and tried to ignore the epilepsy-inducing music.

Solange saw me from across the room. She walked over, a thin grin creeping across her face. "I just spoke with the art critic from *El País*," she whispered in my ear.

"Oh, yeah? What's the verdict?"

She grabbed the pastry from my hand and took a bite. "Impressive, exciting, and energetic," she said, still chewing but savoring every word.

"Nothing about the functioning toilets in the ladies' room?"

She smiled. "Andrew, you know your job is to draw attention to the art, not to the space. And no one does it better than you."

"Thanks."

"And I am sorry I have been such a dictator these last few days," she continued, eating my dinner. "I have never worked for this museum board before. Most of my clients, they are in France and Belgium. So this was new and—"

"Say no more. I understand. With a new client, there's a zero margin of error."

"Exactly," she said. "And for a while, it looked like the whole thing was going to go *pouf!* Tumbling down. And then when the caterer quit on Sunday, I thought I would have the nervous breakdown."

"Right," I said, remembering one of the few problems that wasn't mine to solve. "You didn't ask the caterer to miss his father's funeral, did you?"

She smiled and wiped a dusting of powdered sugar from

her lips. "No. I have the wonderful friend who just happens to be a chef. It is my luck that she was on vacation in Paris."

"That's not luck," I said. "That's kismet."

"What is the *kismet*?" Solange asked, making a face.

Just then, a strangely familiar-looking woman walked past us carrying a tray.

"Solange," she said, "you know what *kismet* is."

"I do?" Solange said. "Remind me."

"It means fate or destiny," the woman said.

"Of course," Solange replied. "My brain has gone to merde. Daisy, you have met Andrew Nelson, the designer of the space? Andrew, this is Daisy Sprinkle. She made the . . . what do you call this?"

"Gooey butter cake," the woman said, smiling. "Nice to meet you."

Even her voice was beautiful. Her hair was swept up. She was wearing a black silk blouse and the same wide-legged black slacks she'd worn on the plane.

Was it possible she didn't recognize me? Had she really not seen me bump her arm while boarding?

I smiled back. "Nice to meet you."

"I'm sorry to interrupt," she said. Then turning to Solange, she added: "Can I borrow your cell phone again? I want to check on Coco."

CHAPTER 32

Daisy

"Non, non, et non," Solange said. "You will not call Coco now. It is late. Let the poor child sleep." She turned to the handsome designer and added: "I am the girl's godmother, so I am entitled to an opinion."

"I see," the man said, smiling.

He was tall. Dark hair with flecks of gray. Nice haircut. Friendly eyes. A kind smile. Lean but not skinny. He was wearing a lightweight gray flannel suit with a white shirt. Midfifties, maybe? I was surprised Solange hadn't told me about him.

"I knew it tasted familiar," he said. "I grew up on gooey butter cake. It was practically its own food group in St. Louis. I'd forgotten how delicious it is."

And he was nice, too. Good for Solange.

"Daisy made red velvet cake, too," said Solange. "She is calling it nostalgia predigital cuisine—or something like that."

"What about Rice Krispie treats?" the guy said. "Let's not forget those."

"Oh, God. I *did* forget those," I said, laughing. "And they would've been great. Or maybe not. French marshmallows are a little too good. For Rice Krispie treats, you really need those cheap, rubbery marshmallows like we have back home." I paused. "I'm sorry, I didn't catch your name?"

"Andrew," he said.

Good name. Solid. Classic. And so much better than Andy.

"And what about mock apple pie?" he asked. "Remember the recipe on the Ritz cracker box?"

"I made that once!" I said. "For my Girl Scout troop."

Now he was laughing. *Nice teeth. God, this guy was adorable. Why hadn't Solange told me about him?* I planned to get Solange in a headlock when we were alone and grill her on her new catch. He was such an improvement over her last boyfriend, Jean Claude, the photographer with an ego the size of Notre Dame.

"Anyway, sorry to interrupt you two," I said again, excusing myself. I had dozens more chocolate-chip cookies in the back room. And my professional waitstaff had professionally disappeared promptly at eleven o'clock.

I walked through the thinning crowd back to the private room Solange had set aside for me. After slipping my hands into plastic gloves, I began arranging the cookies in artful patterns on the empty trays. The door opened.

"Oh, good," I said, not looking up from my work. "At least I've got one waiter left. Let's get rid of these. Just grab any full tray. Tell people to take the cookies home to their kids."

"Oh," a voice said. "All right."

I looked up. It was Andrew.

"Oh, God, I'm sorry!" I said. "I thought you were one of my waiters." I cringed at the thought of what I must look like in the harsh light of the utilitarian room. Haggard and witchy, no doubt. An old bag.

"I can help," Andrew said, smiling.

"No, no," I said. "I really thought you were one of the—"

But he'd already grabbed a tray of cookies.

"Thank you," I said. I grabbed a tray myself and headed back to the dwindling crowd in the reception area. I made a beeline for Solange.

"I cannot *believe* you didn't tell me about Andrew," I whispered. "He's fabulous."

"Yes, he is nice," Solange said distractedly.

"*Nice?* Hello? He's so damn *nice,* I'm jealous."

Solange stared at me. "Jealous? Of what?"

"Of *you,*" I said.

Solange looked puzzled. "Me and Andrew?" Then she smiled. "Daisy, I have been seeing a sculptor named Maria Luciana for six months."

"Maria?" I said. "Luciana?"

"Yes. You'd like her."

I didn't know what to say. Fortunately, we both started cackling at the exact same second.

"You know what?" I finally said. "We don't talk enough anymore, do we?"

"No, we do not," Solange said. "But if you are interested in Andrew, go get him. He is over there, serving your chocolate *chimps.*"

CHAPTER 33

Webb

I somehow forgot about my idea to give Coco a sparkler the first time we kissed. Then again, I hadn't planned on kissing her on both cheeks. I was just going with the flow and following my instincts.

"I can carry that," Coco said, as we were walking out of the train station. She was eyeing her bag.

"Don't be crazy," I said. "I'm the guy."

I was trying to sound funny and macho, but it fell flat. *Less instinct,* I thought. *More thinking. Think before talking.*

"Do you have anything special you want to see?" Coco asked. "Or do you want to just wander around?"

"Um, well . . ." *Should I let her lead the way? Or should I tell her what I want to see?*

"Is the Eiffel Tower cool?" I asked.

"Umm," she said, running her hands through her shiny

brown hair. "You know it's kind of a tourist trap, right? When it was first built, Parisians hated it and wanted it torn down."

"Serious?" I said. "I didn't know that. Okay, what about . . ."

"But if you *want* to see it, we could take the Metro over there. It might be too late to go up in it, but—"

"No, let's . . . um . . ." *Damn. I should've given this whole thing more thought. Why didn't I do a Wiki search on Paris?* "I'm pretty much up for anything. My dad brought me here once when I was like nine or ten, but I don't remember anything."

"My mom did the same thing, when I was even younger," she said. "But I've read all the guidebooks and memorized the maps. Let's take the Metro to Saint Michel and just wander around the Latin Quarter."

"Cool," I said.

Why did everything I say sound so dumb and uninspired?

"We can catch the Metro right over there," Coco said, leading the way. "Oh, wait. What about my bag? You don't want to drag it all over town."

"I don't mind," I said.

Okay, that sounded pathetic. Of course I minded. Just say it! Take charge! Show some initiative.

"Maybe it'd make sense to dump it somewhere," I said.

"Let's go back to the apartment first," Coco said. "You can drop off the bag and . . . you know, whatever."

Huh. Oh. Maybe she wants to have sex now. Just a catch-and-release kind of deal. Hooking up and all that. I guess that'd be okay. I hope she knows how to do it because I sure as hell don't. I mean, c'mon, I'm sure I can figure it out. I've thought about it enough. And if my lamebrain friends can do it, I can, too, right? Right?

"Back to the apartment," I said. "That works for me." I sounded like a slack-brained dolt.

Coco led the way to the Metro station in the bowels of underground Paris. She bought Metro tickets for both of us. She was confident and take-charge. I liked that. But as my body bumped into hers in the Metro car, I felt like an ignorant, inexperienced ten-year-old boy with his older and wiser babysitter.

I remembered what she'd written in one of her e-mails about not wanting a luggage-stealing conviction on her record. She said she needed that like she needed herpes. Okay, so she was definitely experienced. This was good, right? And the herpes part was just a joke, right? Of course it was. No need to ask her about it, right? Right.

"We've got quite a few stops to go," she said as the Metro train lurched forward after a brief stop. It then stopped again suddenly, throwing us together, her feet on mine.

"Monsieur, je vous demande pardon," she said in perfect French. She was laughing. "Je ne l'ai pas fait exprès."

"Huh?"

"Pardon me, monsieur. It was not on purpose," she said. "Marie Antoinette's last words. It's what she supposedly said to her executioner when she stepped on his foot."

"Seriously?" I asked.

Okay, WHY was I such a dumbass? Why didn't I know anything? Why didn't I try harder in school? Why did I take Spanish when it was obvious that girls liked French more?

The train was moving again. I could feel the night getting away from me.

"My shirt looks good on you," I said, trying like hell to sound charming.

"What?" she said, smiling and putting a hand up to her ear.

"My shirt," I repeated, louder. "It looks good on you."

But the sound of the train moving through the tunnel had made conversation impossible.

"*What?*" she asked, louder. She now looked more annoyed than amused.

"Never mind," I mouthed, shaking my head in defeat. I suddenly felt an odd kinship with Marie Antoinette.

I glanced at my watch. Eleven thirty. Seven hours and forty minutes left.

Day 4: Wednesday

Paris

688387

MADRID

Plaza de las Cortes, 7
28014 Madrid

CAMAR SERVER	PERS. PERS.	LOC. LOC.	MESA TABLE	HORA TIME	FECHA DATE	CUENTA No. CHEQUE No.

36/1   11 38

2 @ 8.41
  COPA VINO TINTO
  Subtotal   16.82
  I.V.A.   16.82
  Total   1.18
  Subtotal   18.00
  I.V.A.   16.82
  Pasado   1.18
XXXXXXXXXXXXX073   18.00
9705/MICROS EURO-MA   NXXXX
Euro/Master Card   18.00

CARTE BANCAIRE
Ticket client à conserver

AEROPORT CDG 2
S @. MONTANT ESTIME 16.80 EUR   à 11H32M32
UG 7/1494 r 024 s 5546 no 024024
0119586 000R31680
MONTANT R   EUR

36
+ 17
45
53

CHAPTER 34

Coco

I thought I was reading the signs right, but we took the Metro going the wrong direction—*ack!* It was almost one o'clock in the morning by the time we got back to the apartment.

"This is really cool," Webb said, admiring the walls of Solange's living room.

"Yeah," I agreed. "My godmother's an art freak, as you can tell from all these paintings."

A stretch of awkward silence followed.

"Um," I said, trying to fill the dead air, "do you want something to eat? I picked up some food today at the market."

Actually, I'd spent the whole freakin' day shopping, beginning with the condoms. I'd had to force myself *not* to resent Webb for making me perform this embarrassing task. After all, he really hadn't *made* me do it. He'd probably brought a whole stash of condoms with him. And anyway, why should I be mad at him for wanting to have sex with me? I just hoped he didn't want to start right away. That whole tantric thing was making me nervous.

"I'm starving," he said.

"Perfect!" I said, dashing to the kitchen.

I'd spent hours shopping for the perfect date food. I decided on a baguette from the patisserie, several hunks of cheese from the market, a bunch of grapes (I had to go to a different market for those), and a bottle of wine.

"I hope you like stinky cheese," I said, casually presenting him with the dazzling array of *fromage* I'd spent hours selecting and arranging on one of Solange's prettiest plates.

"Stinky cheese?" he asked, wrinkling his nose.

Oh, God. He was 100 percent adorable. I was finally getting a chance to look at him while he looked at the cheese. Not only was he adorable, he was also handsome. Not like a kid in school, but like a *man*.

"The French love their stinky cheese," I said. "My mom's really into this stuff. She always buys stinky cheese in Chicago, but it's nothing like the cheese you can get in France. Here, try this."

I spread a slice of the baguette with Epoisses and passed it to him. He popped it in his mouth. Then I made one for myself.

"This was supposedly Napoleon's favorite cheese," I said between bites. "It's made from raw cow's milk. Do you like it?"

He chewed and smiled.

"Try this one," I continued, loading up a thin slice of bread with a thick layer of Camembert. "My mom is nutso for this stuff. She thinks it's the best cheese in the world. The French say Camembert tastes like God's feet. Isn't that hilarious?"

He put it in his mouth and smiled again.

"You probably recognize this one," I said. "Roquefort. The blue, of course, is mold. Here you go."

I smeared some on a piece of bread and passed it to him. He took a big bite.

"It comes from a small village in southern France," I explained. *Why did I suddenly sound like my mother?* "The milk isn't pasteurized, so there's a risk of *Listeria* infection, which, get this, can be deadly in some people and cause pregnant women to lose their babies."

Okay, WHY was I talking about pregnancy and babies? He was going to think I wanted to get pregnant. And why wasn't he saying anything? Was it because I was talking like a madwoman who wouldn't shut up? No. I was leaving plenty of airtime for him to jump in and say something. But he was just sitting there, eating and smiling weirdly at me. Was he thinking about sex? Was he a sex maniac? Was cheese like oysters—one of those hormone-charged delicacies that turns men on? Did he think I was trying to turn him on? Shit, shit, shit, shit.

"If you like those, you should try Stinking Bishop," I pressed on, trying to make it clear that this was really about cheese, not sex. "I saw some Stinking Bishop in Solange's fridge. She wouldn't mind if you try some. Wait right there."

I ran the four steps to the kitchen. Webb remained in the living room, plotting God knows what. "You know what's really funny about these stinky cheeses?" I yammered on from the kitchen. "Some of them, like Epoisses, smell so foul you're not even supposed to carry them with you on public transportation. Isn't that funny? Ha ha. HA!"

I was rifling through Solange's refrigerator, looking for the Stinking Bishop. I grabbed it, along with a big knife, just in case. *I don't even know this guy! If he tries something weird, I'll just wave the knife ninja-style and pretend I know what I'm doing.*

"Coco?" Webb asked from the living room in a strange voice.

"Yeah," I said, closing my eyes and wishing I was in a computer cubicle, talking to him online.

"Can I have something to drink?"

CHAPTER 35

Andrew

I had to tell her. It was just too ludicrous. What were the mathematical odds?

I watched her from across the exhibit space. She was talking to Solange. They were laughing.

God, she's beautiful. The blue lights only accentuated her angles. Here she looked less like a Botticelli and more like a Modigliani painted in cobalt hues.

I should tell her about the note. I *had* to tell her. Maybe I'd write something clever on a napkin and put it on her tray.

Enough with the secret notes already.

But wouldn't she find the whole thing amusing, even though she'd called me a first-class ass? Well, I *was* an ass. Who but an ass hides a note in a woman's purse? But now that she knew me, she'd see how funny the whole thing was.

She was walking toward me with a tray of cookies. She was smiling. I smiled back.

"I think we're the only two still working," Daisy said over the techno music that had ceased to bother me.

"The few, the proud, the brave," I said.

She laughed a deep, honest laugh. *God, what a great laugh.*

"I hate for all this to go to waste," she said, looking at the tray. "And I've got dozens more cookies in the back. At home I always make sure the leftovers go to a food pantry or a women's shelter."

"That's wonderful," I said. *She's not only beautiful, but thoughtful and socially conscious. She's perfect.*

"Do you think I should box these up and take them back for the housekeeping staff at my hotel?" she asked. "I'm sure they all have families."

"Great idea," I said. "Where are you staying?"

"The Palace."

"Same here." *This was fate. This was meant to be.* "Let me help you."

"Please, no," she said, laughing. "You've gone beyond the call of duty. Solange tells me you've been working around the clock getting this show ready."

"Solange exaggerates," I said. "Besides, I'm running on fumes now. Give me just a minute or two. I'll meet you in the back."

"Okay, then," she said. "Thanks." She smiled again and turned on her heel.

I put the tray of cookies down on the nearest flat surface and checked my BlackBerry for messages from Webb. I hadn't seen him all night, but he'd been terrific about e-mailing me. I had an unread message sent at 12:36 A.M.

Fr: Webbn@com
To: Lineman@com
Subject: g/night

Cool show! Congrats. You were busy talking to people,
so I didn't want to bother you. I just got back to the
hotel. Going to bed now. Are u still planning on sleeping
late tmw? Me too. Let's not wake each other, OK?

Perfect. The planets were in alignment. Fate was on my side.

I found Daisy back in the prep room, boxing up cookies
and gooey butter cake squares. In my mind I rehearsed how
I'd tell her. *Did you by any chance find a note in your purse
when you arrived in Paris?* Strike that. *Hey, what would you
say if I told you I was the ass who slipped that pickup note in
your purse?* No. What about: *How strange. I just got an e-mail
from a woman who called me a first-class ass. What do you make
of that?*

Why was I trying to sabotage myself like this? Why tell her
at all?

Because I had to.

Okay, but how about twenty-five years from now when we
could have a good laugh about it?

I watched her slide rows of cookies neatly into boxes.

She looked up. "You're staring. Do I have chocolate on my
face or something? God, I'm a mess."

"No," I said. "Just the opposite."

CHAPTER 36

Daisy

$\mathcal{I}$'m convinced Solange tried to push me into Andrew on the front steps of the Crystal Palace.

"Andrew, you will see that Daisy gets back to the hotel, yes?" Solange asked.

"I will," he said, holding boxes of cookies in his hands.

He's adorable. He looks like a little boy carrying a cafeteria tray.

"Good," Solange said, winking at me. "Because I am staying at Maria Luciana's tonight.

Maria Luciana. Who knew?

"But Daisy," Solange continued, "I am taking you to the airport tomorrow morning."

"Absolutely not," I said. "I'll get a cab. My flight's at seven o'clock. There's no reason for you to get up that early. Aren't you coming to Chicago next month, anyway?"

"I am," Solange confirmed. "We will catch up then?"

"Yes," I said. "Perfect."

Solange hugged me and performed a yoga bow for Andrew.

"I am hopelessly in debt for all you did to make this show happen. Really, I am in debt to *both* of you."

"I'll remember that," Andrew said.

"Good night," I added as we started down the steps. I stopped. "Wait! I forgot to give you your cell phone."

I put my box of sweets on the top step and began digging through my purse.

"Keep it," Solange called over her shoulder. "I have a half-dozen phones. Use it while you're in Paris. You can give it to me when I'm in Chicago."

"*Really?*"

"Really. Good-bye!" Solange blew kisses as Andrew and I walked down the crushed gravel path that led to the gates of Retiro Park.

"Why are these things always so exhausting?" I asked.

"I was just wondering the same thing," Andrew said. "I'm getting too old for this."

I wondered how old he might be. Early fiftysomething, I imagined. He didn't wear a wedding ring, but that was no guarantee he was single. Still, it was a good sign, just like his kind offer to help me serve cookies. I suddenly regretted my early morning flight. It would've been nice to compare notes about the show over a lazy breakfast.

We walked side by side under a dark canopy of trees toward the park entrance. From a distance, I could see people on the street. They were carrying signs.

"Are those protesters?" I asked.

"I have no idea," Andrew said, staring ahead at the assembled crowd.

"Look. The signs are cut to resemble hands."

"Cinco por Cinco," Andrew said, reading the words on the sign.

"Five for five?" I asked. "What does it mean?"

A teenage couple was sitting on a park bench, watching the protesters.

"¿Qué pasa con ellos?" Andrew asked.

"Manifestación," said the boy emphatically. "Cinco por Cinco. Son locos." He made the international sign for crazy by turning his index finger in circles next to his head.

"Do you think they've been marching like that all night?" I asked Andrew. "My feet hurt just looking at them."

He smiled and switched places with me so that he was walking closest to the protesters when we passed them. They were dressed in black. The men, mostly in their twenties and thirties, had longish beards and wore black hats. The women were dressed in skirts and shawls. Up close they looked harmless, almost like the Mennonites who sold apples at the Oak Park farmers' market.

Andrew and I walked in silence for a few moments.

"I wish you didn't have to leave so early tomorrow," he finally said.

Really? Did he wish this for his sake or mine? Or was he just making conversation? I thought I detected a note of sincere disappointment in his voice.

"I have to get back," I answered. "I left my daughter there, at Solange's apartment. She was feeling too sick to make the trip."

Oh, God. That makes me sound like a horrible parent.

"She's eighteen," I clarified.

"Ah," he said. "I have a son. Seventeen."

So he was married. Oh, well. Damn. Shit.

"I've barely seen him since we got here," he continued, almost like a confession.

"Is he spending time with . . . your wife?" I asked. "Or, um, your partner?"

I was never this bold. But I was tired, and my flight was leaving in six hours. And, while I couldn't explain it, I felt a connection to this guy.

Or am I just tired? I know I need a small vacation.

"Just me and Webb," Andrew said.

"Oh!" I said with way too much enthusiasm. I tried again, less peppy this time. "Just the two of you. That's . . . nice."

He was large but gentle: a rare combination in nature. My mind inexplicably flew back to an old chef in culinary school who had repeatedly lectured about how the youngest meat is always the most desirous. It never failed to elicit bemused looks from his students, both male and female.

Fifteen minutes later we were back at the hotel. Andrew watched as I filled the arms of two confused bellhops with boxes of sugary predigital treats. I tried to explain in my best high school Spanish that I wanted them to give the food away to their fellow workers.

"Do you think they understood me?" I asked Andrew when we were standing in the lobby.

"I'm not sure I understand you. But I'd like to. Would it be foolish of me to ask if you'd care for a drink?"

"I'd love one," I said.

I looked at my watch: 2:05 A.M.

CHAPTER 37

Webb

As soon as Coco was in the kitchen, I spit the vomitous cheese in my hand.

"Do you want wine or soda or water or . . ." she called.

What I wanted was *time*. And a place to dump the cheese guano I'd held in my mouth for as long as humanly possible.

"Uh, do you have any hot tea?" I asked, grimacing even as I said the words. *Hot tea?* Surely she was more enlightened than my idiot guy friends who equated drinking tea with being gay.

"Oh, sure," she said brightly from the kitchen. "Solange has all kinds of teas. I love tea, too!"

Suddenly Coco was back in the living room, holding a wooden box filled with tea bags. I hid the cheese in my fist.

"Pick a tea, any tea," she said, smiling.

"Uh, let's see. Chamomile sounds good," I said, handing

her the first bag I saw. I had to use my left hand because my right hand held the half-chewed flotsam.

"That might put you to sleep," she said tentatively.

Did that mean she wanted to go to bed with me?

"You're right," I said. "Well then, *mon ami,* I'll just have whatever you're having."

"I really like Earl Grey," she said.

Is that a double entendre? Is Earl Grey code for a certain kind of sex? I can't think straight with the aftertaste of poisonous cheese festering in my mouth.

"Excellent," I said, trying to sound chipper.

While she returned to the kitchen to make the tea, I scanned the room to find a place to stash the cheese.

"This'll just take a sec," she hollered.

"Take your time!"

I could've tried to sprint to the bathroom and dump the vile stuff down the toilet, but I'd have to pass the kitchen. Wouldn't I look suspicious hiding something in my hand? Plus, unless I banked the cheese off the side of the toilet, there'd be a huge *plop* accompanied by a hideous smell. She'd think I'd just taken a foul dump.

"Do you want sugar or honey in your tea?" she asked.

"Yes, honey," I said.

Ugh! Think before you talk, idiot!

"These electric kettles really heat up fast," she was saying from the kitchen. "And I think they're, like, super energy efficient. I wonder why people don't use them back home. Do you know?"

"Uh-huh," I said. "I mean, no."

She was still rattling around in the kitchen. I had to think fast.

I could hide the stinky cheese behind a stack of books on a shelf. But the smell would give it—and me—away in no time.

There was only one solution. My duffel bag was sitting near a futon against the wall. If I could just stash the cheese in my bag, I'd deal with it later. I'd dump it down the toilet on the train or throw it out the window or something. Anything. I just had to get rid of it.

I felt myself levitating above the scene, distancing myself from the horror of it all. It was almost as if I was watching myself from above as I moved slowly across the room. I opened the side pocket of my bag and slid the handful of cheese deep inside the tight space.

I was just withdrawing my hand from the bag when Coco returned to the living room carrying two mugs of tea.

"I hope you like—" she began. And then she stopped. "What the hell are you doing in my bag?"

CHAPTER 38

Coco

$\mathcal{I}$ could tell Webb was sorry.

"I thought this was my bag," he said, putting one hand to his forehead. "I am such a moron."

"Don't worry about it," I said, handing him his tea. "Seriously, no big deal. Do you need to get something from my bag?"

"Uh, no," he said, looking a bit dazed. "I just . . . um. I'll deal with it later."

"Okay." I blew on my tea and then took a sip.

Silence.

He took a sip.

More silence.

"Do you want to wander around after this?" he asked.

"Sure," I answered.

Okay, so he didn't want to have tantric sex with me. Fine. Great. Whatever. That was okay. Maybe it was for the best.

"I should take my camera," I said. "I haven't been able to take any pictures since we got here."

I set my cup down on the floor and reached over to grab my bag. I pulled the top zipper, but gasped in horror at what I saw.

"What's wrong?" he asked, kneeling to see what I was staring at.

I reached across and pushed him back on his ass so he couldn't see what I saw. "Nothing!" I said frantically. "It's nothing!"

"Did I wrinkle your clothes?" he asked. "Do I need to buy you a new wardrobe or something?"

He was being sweet. He was pretending not to notice. But how could he *possibly* have missed the pink padded bra that practically *jumped* out of the bag when I unzipped it?

"I *told* you not to look through my stuff," I snapped.

"I didn't," he said. "I mean, I *had* to look through some of it to see it wasn't mine. But besides that—"

"Never mind," I said. "I don't want to talk about it."

And I didn't. But I could've *murdered* my mother for telling me to pack my oldest, most worn-out underwear. Bringing old underwear and bras to Paris and replacing them with new stuff had sounded okay at the time. But that was a week ago! And now Webb had seen my faded old flowered granny panties and stretched-out foam-padded bras, which I hadn't worn for over a year if not *longer* because they were god-awful to begin with and also because the padding had turned all lumpy and tumory.

I felt like screaming at the top of my lungs: *If you think I wear foam-padded bras, I don't! Right now I'm wearing a gorgeous midnight blue silk bra and matching undies from Galeries Lafayette that would drive you mad with desire, if only you knew!*

But of course I couldn't say that. No wonder he didn't want to have tantric sex with me.

I grabbed my camera from the bag, trying not to cry. "Let's just go," I said blankly.

"Seriously, do I need to buy you new clothes or something?" he asked. "Did I fold them wrong or, I don't know, *contaminate* them somehow?"

I laughed weakly. "Don't worry about it. Let's just get out of here."

So we left the apartment and walked around Solange's neighborhood.

"We could walk to Sacré Coeur," I said. "It's pretty close."

"That'd be great," he said.

We walked in silence for about a block.

"Coco's a really cool name," he said.

"My mom lived in Paris for a while. She went to culinary school here and studied with a pastry chef. She's wild for chocolate."

"As in cocoa?" he said.

"Yep. And she loves her designer clothes, especially Chanel. It's a brand that was started by Coco Chanel."

"Plus," he said, "it's just a cool word to say: *Coco*."

"I think Webb's a cool name."

"Now you're just being polite, Blouse Girl."

"No, I really do. But I don't know anything about Jimmy Webb."

"I bet you know his songs. He had some hits in the seventies."

"Like what?"

"His most famous song was 'Wichita Lineman.' It was a big hit for Glen Campbell."

"I've never heard of Glen Campbell," I admitted. "Or that song."

"Sure you have," he said, and he began singing into an invisible microphone as we walked down the narrow sidewalk:

I am a lineman for the county and I drive the main road
Searchin' in the sun for another overload.
I hear you singin' in the wire, I can hear you through
*   the whine*
And the Wichita Lineman is still on the liiiiiiiiiiiiiiiiiiine.

I couldn't stop laughing. He almost made me forget my stupid pink foam bra. Almost.

"That," I said between laughs, "is the funniest thing I've ever heard in my life. But I don't understand the lyrics. Is it about a phone repair guy listening to a woman talk on the phone? He can hear her singing through the wire? Who's he listening to? Is he a stalker?"

"No idea," he said. "The second verse is even weirder."

"Sing it," I said.

"Sorry," he replied. He seemed embarrassed now. I shouldn't have laughed.

"But I really want to hear it," I said. "Please?"

"It's not fair to Jimmy Webb," he said. Then he pointed across the street. "Is that Internet café open? Let's go look it up on YouTube."

So we bought an hour's worth of time and found Glen Campbell singing "Wichita Lineman." We listened closely to the lyrics of the second verse:

> *And I need you more than want you, and I want you*
> *for all time.*
> *And the Wichita Lineman is still on the line.*

"He needs her more than wants her?" I asked. "Isn't that sort of an insult?"

"I know," Webb said. "Can't you just picture an old guy in a terrible marriage? But he doesn't know how to cook or where to find the clean towels, so he's stuck with her."

"But he wants her for all time," I said. "That doesn't make sense."

"Unless he likes needing her?" Webb suggested.

"Which makes him a codependent loser," I said. *Why was I making fun of Webb's namesake's song?* "The melody is really pretty, though."

"Yeah," Webb said. "There's something haunting about it. Listen to this."

He downloaded a clip of R.E.M's Michael Stipe singing "Wichita Lineman."

"It's pretty but sad," I said when the song ended. "It's like the guy's in love, but there's something missing. Why is he still on the line? I don't get it."

"Me neither," he said. "Jimmy Webb also wrote 'MacArthur Park.' "

I shrugged. "Never heard of it."

"It's the world's most stupid song. It begins 'Someone left the cake out in the rain.' "

"Oh, wait!" I shrieked. "I do know that song. It was a big disco song, right?"

We watched a YouTube video of Donna Summer singing it and howled. The guy at the computer next to us raised his eyebrows.

"We have to be quiet," I said.

"Hold on," Webb whispered. "You gotta see this." He downloaded a video of Sammy Davis Jr. singing "MacArthur Park." Then we watched Andy Williams sing it. And then Diana Ross. The Four Tops. Maynard Ferguson. Tony Bennett.

I was weak from laughing so hard. The guy next to us left, muttering something in French.

Webb slid over to the abandoned computer and typed, *This PC is infected. Please use another.*

"What're you doing?" I whispered.

"Just wait," he said. He highlighted the words and translated them into French. "There. Now no one will bug us."

God, he's cool.

"You're diabolical," I said.

"Possibly," he acknowledged. Then he bowed to me. "But my Blouse Girl needs her space." He smiled. "Hey, this is almost like a date, y'know?"

"I know!" I said.

He went to the front counter and bought more computer time. When he returned, he downloaded Liza Minnelli singing "MacArthur Park." He took my hands in his and sang along with the words while staring into my eyes. " 'I don't think that I can make it, 'cause it took so long to bake it. And I'll never have that recipe again. *Agaaaiiinnn.*' "

"It's insane," I said. "What makes it so funny is how seriously they sing it. It's just nonsense right? I mean, who in the name of God would leave a cake out in the rain?"

We found more Jimmy Webb songs online, including "Up Up and Away."

"I've heard this one," I said. "Up, up and away in my beautiful balloon."

"It's about condoms," Webb said.

"It *is?*"

"That's what I heard."

"Ick," I said. "Gross."

Why was I sounding like such a prude?

"Show me your school," he said, switching gears. So I pulled up my school's website and took him on a virtual tour. He seemed impressed by the history of the school and the fact that my mom and grandparents had all gone there. Then I showed him some of the restaurants where my mom had worked. I also showed him our neighborhood association site, which had a picture of our house on it.

"Okay, enough about me," I said. "Your turn."

He downloaded his school's website and clicked on the faculty page. Then he proceeded to tell me about all his teachers, including his favorite English teacher, Miss Fogerty, and his driver's ed teacher, who was a perv.

"Oh my God," I said. "Ours is a perv, too."

"Seriously? You think it's part of the job description?"

Webb asked. "Our guy is so bad, I refused to take driver's ed. I sent an e-mail to the principal, saying I was boycotting the class until they found a teacher who didn't sexually harass the girls."

"That's so sweet," I said. "So did you have to go to a private driving school?"

"Nah. I just skipped the whole driver's license thing."

"You skipped getting a *driver's license*?"

"Yeah, I'd rather walk or take public transportation," he said.

What a cool guy. Who cares if he's seen my stupid pink foam-padded bra?

I clicked back to my school's website so I could show him a picture of our driver's ed teacher. We howled at how much they looked alike.

"We should take pictures of ourselves," I said.

I held the camera out in front of us and snapped pictures of Webb and me with his school's driver's ed teacher in the background. Then I took one of us with my driver's ed teacher.

"Let's get one with Glen Campbell," he said.

"Brilliant!" I said.

I'm not even thinking about my stupid pink bra!

He downloaded a video of Glen and played it while I set up the shot.

"Perfect," I said. "We should get a picture in front of the Eiffel Tower. I mean, the real thing."

"Great idea," Webb said. "Do we have time?"

"What time is it? I don't have my iPhone."

"I don't have my phone, either," he said. "How do we find out . . . oh wait. Duh."

He leaned in close to the computer and looked at the tiny clock in the lower right corner. "It's almost three o'clock. My train leaves at ten after seven."

"No problem," I said. "I know how to get back to Gare de Lyon."

He made a face. "Crap, I think I'm leaving from a different station. Gare de . . . something."

"They're all *gare de* something," I said. "*Gare* is French for *station*."

He slung his arm around my shoulder and whispered in my ear. "Mademoiselle Blouse is *zee* brilliant *ingénue*." He paused. "Hey, am I speaking French?"

"No," I said, laughing. "Where's monsieur's train schedule?"

He searched his pockets. "It's here somewhere. Oh wait."

"What?"

"I think I put it in your bag. Which is back at the apartment."

"Which is where your bag is, too," I said, laughing. "We better go back to Solange's and figure out how to get to your train station."

No need to tell him it had taken me an hour to figure out how to get to Gare de Lyon by Metro, and still I'd screwed up the return trip.

"C'mon," he said. "I'll race you."

And before I knew it, there we were, hand in hand, running back to Solange's apartment, singing Jimmy Webb songs and laughing like fools.

CHAPTER 39

Andrew

Daisy and I found a small corner table in the wood-paneled hotel bar. After we ordered drinks, I excused myself to check on Webb.

"Everything okay?" Daisy asked when I returned.

"Asleep," I reported. "Under a mountain of blankets."

Should I confess my frustration with Webb? Would it be a betrayal of my son—or might Daisy have some insight into the minds of teenagers?

"He spends so much time in front of the damn computer," I said, leaping recklessly into the subject of adolescent children. "I worry like hell he's becoming antisocial. He has such . . . inertia. Even here, he's spending hours in front of a computer, playing games. Or whatever they do."

"My daughter's the same way," she said, taking a sip of wine. "But you know, I don't think it's all bad. With Coco—and I'm sure it's the same with your son—they have friends all over the world because of these online groups and forums they join."

"Right," I agreed. "But can you really call those *friendships*? I'm not sure I buy all this connecting online stuff. It was like that museum show. Digital love depresses the hell out of me."

Wait. Why was I being so negative? The bad bourbon was going straight to my head. Why did the Spanish import only the cheapest American bourbon? I should've eaten dinner. I should eat some olives and nuts. They're on the table. That's what they're for.

I grabbed a handful of nuts and then dropped most of them. Daisy laughed. It was a deep, unself-conscious laugh, and it made her even more beautiful. She was the kind of woman who would grow more beautiful with age. I'd never understand why women tried to hide those pretty little laugh lines around their eyes.

"My son doesn't even know how to make eye contact with people," I said, sighing. "Maybe I shouldn't be so hard on him. But we're in Europe. Shouldn't he be falling in love with some local girl he meets in a plaza—or at least admiring someone from afar?"

No need to mention slipping notes in the bags of attractive women one sees on planes.

"European romances can be overrated," Daisy said, popping an olive in her mouth.

"You sound like you have some experience in that department."

She looked at me and narrowed her eyes, as if wondering whether to explain herself.

"My daughter," she finally said, "was conceived when I was in Paris attending culinary school."

"Oh," I replied.

"Yeah," she said, her eyes widening.

"And . . . how'd that work out, if it's not too personal to ask?"

"It was complicated," she said. "He was a pastry chef. A master chef. He seemed happy when I told him I was pregnant. But he said he could never be monogamous."

"Oh," I said again.

"Yeah," she said, smiling. "*Oh.*"

"At least he was honest?" I tried.

"At least," she said. "Please, this is all ancient history. And so boring. I really can't even remember the details. I have a weird kind of relationship Alzheimer's."

"Relationship Alzheimer's?"

"Just what it sounds like. I forget everything as soon as it's over. But one thing I do remember: after he told me, it made the whole thing easier for me. Because I knew I didn't want to raise a child with him or marry him—not that he asked."

"Sounds like a first-class ass," I said.

WHY did I just say that? She's going to connect the dots. She knows. Or she will know. Why did I write that stupid goddamn note on the plane?! Wait. She's talking. Listen to her, you first-class ass!

"Does he keep in touch with you or your daughter?" I asked.

"No," she answered. "Oh wait, he did send her a porcelain doll and a card for her fifth birthday."

"Hmm," I offered. "Too little too late?"

"You could say that," Daisy replied. "Especially because she was seven at the time." She smiled and shook her head at the memory. "I'm glad I had the sense to walk away from that. I'm pretty good at walking away from things—probably too good, in fact."

"Well, you've got to know when to leave a bad situation."

"Yes," she agreed, toasting me with her wineglass. "Would you believe I just walked away from a job at the best restaurant in Chicago because of steak sauce?"

"Steak sauce?"

"Terrible stuff," she said. "Just thickened sugar water, really. The owner wanted to have some in the back. You know, in case someone wanted *steak sauce*."

She said it like it was hemlock.

"And you said . . ."

"I said, 'Fine. Have your damn steak sauce. I'm leaving.'" She took a sip. "That was a week ago today."

"Sorry," I said.

She waved a hand as if batting away a fly. "Not at all. I was finished there. I left the restaurant before that over a TV."

"As in, a television?" I asked.

"Yes. The owner of this wonderful restaurant decided to cover one wall in the bar with flat-screen TVs." She looked around the bar we were sitting in. "Have you noticed that Europeans aren't as TV crazy as Americans?"

"Maybe because they don't need the distraction of televised sporting events," I said, deciding my particular obsession with the St. Louis Cardinals could wait to be explained later. "Europeans know how to have conversations."

"Exactly," she said. "What's wrong with just talking? Isn't that why bars were invented? So you could talk to somebody over a drink—as opposed to sitting at home alone getting sloshed?"

I loved how frank she was. I loved her smile. Her face. All those emotions swirling between her eyes and mouth. There was a tension that made me want to hear more, even though I didn't fully understand her. Her face asked questions and made me care. Here I'd been thinking she was a Modigliani, but I was wrong. She was a Jimmy Webb song.

"Tell me about your daughter," I said. "Her name's Coco—as in Chanel?"

"Very good," Daisy said, smiling. "I'm a big admirer of hers."

"I don't know very much about her," I said.

"Let's see," Daisy began. "She learned how to sew in an orphanage. She was a survivor from the very beginning. She had a million obstacles, but ultimately she succeeded because she worked like a dog, and because she had the revolutionary idea that women should dress for themselves and not for men. She never married, which was unusual back then. That, combined with everything else, led her to be seen as a new kind of woman—one who could be independent, successful, and stylish."

"Sounds familiar," I said, raising a glass to my drinking companion.

Even in the dim light I could see her face redden. A woman who blushes. What would Coco Chanel say?

"I guess what I like most about her," Daisy continued, "was that she made simplicity beautiful. It sounds like a no-brainer, but it was huge back then. It's still huge now. How many times have you been to a supposedly good restaurant where you can't even taste the food because it's covered in . . . innovation?"

I couldn't help smiling.

"You know what I mean," she insisted. "Carrot soup should taste like carrots. Roast chicken should taste like chicken. A lemon tart should taste like lemons. All these so-called postmodern chefs with their delusions of creativity. It makes me cranky."

I felt surprisingly relaxed with this woman, but there was something else. Something pleasantly unsettling. *Passion.* It's what the museum show had lacked.

"I have a feeling you and Ms. Chanel would've gotten along famously," I said.

"You're kind," she said. "But a strong, self-reliant character is important. It's what I want my daughter to have. But you know what they say: careful what you wish for."

"What do you mean?"

"Oh, God," she said, shaking her head. "My daughter is completely independent. Eighteen years old and ready to run the world. She has no use for me anymore."

"That's wonderful," I said. "I'm trying to do the same thing with my son. I want him to live without worrying what I think or what anyone thinks. I want him to have high standards for himself."

"Yes," she agreed. "That's important. But Coco's so hard on herself. I don't know what she'll do if she ever gets a B. She goes into hysterics if she gets an A minus. That's not good. Life's not like that."

"No, it's not."

"I try to get her to come with me to Paris every year," she said. "But she never wants to miss school. She hasn't been to Paris with me since she was eight—by *her* choice, not mine. Can you imagine?"

"No. Webb's always looking for an excuse to miss school."

"The only reason she came with me on this trip was because I was able to plan it around her spring break. She wants to be perfect. It's a recipe for disaster."

"Or at least unhappiness."

"Exactly," she said. "And you know, that's another reason I named her Coco. Because to me, chocolate is about indulging in things that give you pleasure. And what's the point of life if you can't find joy?"

On that note, we ordered another round of drinks.

"How'd you end up with a boy named Webb?" she asked. "Is there a story behind it?"

"There is, but it's a long one."

She looked at her watch: "I have almost four hours until my flight leaves."

CHAPTER 40

Daisy

"A re you sure you want to hear this?" Andrew asked, smiling wearily.

I would've preferred a long, inconsequential story so I could stop listening and simply study his face. But this didn't sound like one of those stories.

"Of course I want to hear it," I said. "Dish."

He smiled. *What a sweet smile. What a good man.*

"Okay," he said, turning more serious. "I'm the father of my sister's child."

What the—?

"Not the biological father," he said quickly. "I adopted Webb when he was born. From my sister, Laura."

"She didn't want a baby?" I asked.

He took a thoughtful sip before answering. "She belonged to a cult. It's a complicated story, but no, she didn't want a baby. Or the cult leader didn't want a baby. He was the father."

"Oh, jeez," I said. "What a jerk. But how wonderful that you were willing to adopt."

"No white horse here," he said. "The truth is, I probably didn't give it enough thought. I was thirty-six years old at the time."

I stopped listening and started calculating. *Thirty-six plus seventeen equals . . . What does it equal? I need a pen and paper. Think! 36 + 17 = 43. Is that right? No, idiot. Carry the one. Fifty-three. He's fifty-three. How old am I? Forty-four? No, forty-five. Nine-year difference? No, eight! God, am I drunk or just stupid? Shut up and listen!*

"Uh-huh," I said, checking back into the conversation.

"Laura knew the baby was going to be a boy. And I figured, I could do that. I knew boy stuff. And there was nobody else. I'm her only sibling. So I took him home from the hospital."

"Go on," I said.

"I guess that's why I worry about Webb becoming dependent on anyone or anything—like the damn computer. Laura is probably the most naturally gifted abstract painter I've ever known. But she somehow managed to rob a bank and kill two tellers for her so-called boyfriend, the cult leader. He got three years. She got twenty-five."

"Jesus Christ," I said.

"I know. So that's why I'm always searching in my son for another overload."

"I'm . . . sorry." I started to reach across the table and put my hand on his. But he'd already clasped his hands behind his head and was stretching backward.

"Please," he said. "I'm the one who should apologize. I don't tell many people. It's a story that can clear a room."

"I'm assuming your son knows about all this?"

"Not every detail, but he knows." He paused. "Shall we change the subject?"

"Of course," I said. I felt an irrational fondness for this man wash over me. "But can you tell me about the name 'Webb'? I like it."

His face brightened. "I named him after my favorite songwriter, Jimmy Webb."

I cringed. "I should know him, right?"

"You probably do, but you don't know you know him," he said generously. "He's sort of like your friend, Coco Chanel. Jimmy Webb wasn't an orphan, but he came from humble roots in Oklahoma. His dad was a Baptist minister who didn't think much of his son's plans to be a songwriter. The father allowed only white gospel music and country music in their home. But when it was clear that making music was what Jimmy really wanted to do, his father gave him forty bucks and said, 'It's not much, but it's all I have.' He also told his son that writing songs would break his heart."

"Whose heart—the father's or the son's?" I asked.

"The son's," he said. "Jimmy's heart."

"Oh, that's so sad. But also great."

"I agree. Because that's what art is; that's what it does. It breaks your heart. It moves you. If it doesn't do that, forget it. It's not worth it."

He had an artist's heart, but none of the weird artist hang-ups, like being broke. He was kind. He was generous. He had lovely manners. His face was warm in the candlelight. I couldn't help hoping that my face looked softer and less haggard in the bar light than it had in that hideous workroom at the museum.

"What about the exhibit tonight?" I asked. "Did it move you?"

"Not especially," he said. "But I'm not the target demographic for shows like that. I prefer paintings."

We talked about art museums we loved. He knew them all but was wonderfully unsnobbish about it. Such a nice change from the poseurs who visited the Art Institute once a year and considered themselves *arty*.

"Of course, the museums in Europe are spectacular," he was saying. "And you have the Art Institute in Chicago, which is wonderful. But the museums I find myself enjoying most are in Kansas City, Tulsa, Toledo, Ohio."

"Tell *that* to a New Yorker," I mumbled.

"They wouldn't believe me," he said. "It's like admitting Glen Campbell is your favorite singer."

"*Is* he?"

"Yes." He laughed. "And now you know everything about me. But really, how can you beat his stuff: 'Wichita Lineman,' 'By the Time I Get to Phoenix,' 'Gentle on My Mind'?"

"Now that last one I remember," I said. "I used to think it sounded so romantic, letting a guy leave his sleeping bag rolled up and stashed behind your couch. Now I think, for God's sake, buddy. Get it together and get a bed. Get a house. Stop trashing my place."

He laughed, but sadly. *Oh God, I've offended him.*

"That's exactly what I worry about with my son," he said. "That he'll be a guy who leaves his sleeping bag rolled up behind some poor girl's couch."

"But at a certain age, that *does* sound romantic," I said. "To women as much as men."

"Maybe it's an analog thing," he said.

I took a chance. "I think romance is harder in the digital or postdigital age or whatever we're supposed to call it. *Love* is harder."

"You think so?" he asked.

"I *do*. Don't you see it with your son?"

"My son doesn't date," he said. "Not at all."

"Neither does my daughter. She says dating is for losers. They don't get it. There's no such thing as dinner and a movie anymore."

"They just roam in packs," he added.

"They don't hold hands. Or if they do, it's done with irony and eyeball rolling."

He smiled. "Holding hands. Wouldn't that be digital—you know, literally touching digits?"

"You're right," I said. "I hadn't thought of it like that. So love in the postdigital age is an age where nobody touches? Do you know when I was in college, I dated a guy for a year or so."

"Are you telling me you held this man's hand?" he asked, grinning.

"I did. And during breaks from school, when we couldn't hold hands, we wrote letters—because long-distance calls cost money back then."

He was smiling. "I remember those days."

"And I'll tell you something else," I continued, encouraged by his eyes.

"Tell me," he said.

"We also had this thing where we'd call each other and let the phone ring once, and then hang up. So it wouldn't cost anything. But also because—"

"It was your thing," he said.

"Yes. It was romantic."

Wait, was it romantic? It was so long ago. I could barely remember. It should've been romantic. Was it?

"I get that," he said. "And I like that the guy got credit every time the phone rang once at your house. What if it was a wrong number, and the person on the other end hung up after the first ring when they realized they'd misdialed?"

"I'm not even listening to you," I said, laughing and covering my ears. "I won't let you sully a lovely memory."

His voice softened. "I wouldn't dream of doing that."

We were alone. The bar had closed a half hour earlier. Even the bartender was gone.

"You have a flight to catch," he said, "and here I am keeping you up."

"Oh, it's *no* problem, really," I said, a little too eagerly.

Don't sound so damn pathetic. He'll think I want him to spend the night in my room.

"Want to walk around the neighborhood?" he asked.

"That would be nice."

My body was exhausted from the long afternoon of baking.

And now the wine had made me light-headed. But the night air felt wonderful and warm.

We saw a group of rough-looking boys selling what looked like drug paraphernalia from a card table across the street. Andrew again changed places with me so he was walking next to the street.

"Back to gooey butter cake for a moment," he said.

I laughed.

"No, really," he said. "I don't think you realize what an inspired choice that was. Maybe the people there tonight didn't get it, but to me, gooey butter cake represents analog culture right as it started turning the corner toward digital."

"And why is that?" I asked.

"I don't know. I'm not always good at explaining these things. But I feel them. You'd have to ask Jimmy Webb to explain cakes. He wrote a song about a cake called 'MacArthur Park.'"

"Donna Summer," I said. "Loved her."

"Yes." He sighed. "She did a disco cover of it. But it was originally a Richard Harris song because nobody else would record it. Do you remember it? 'Someone left the cake out in the rain . . .' There's a poem by W. H. Auden with the line, 'My face looks like a wedding cake left out in the rain.'"

I stopped walking and turned toward him. "That's heartbreaking."

"I agree," he said. "Don't you know exactly what he's talking about?"

Yes. Because I've looked like that before. More than once, in fact.

We walked in silence for a block.

"Does Webb visit his mother in prison?" I asked.

"No, but I go. Laura doesn't want Webb to see her like that."

"And when she gets out?"

"Webb will be a grown man. They'll have to forge their own relationship."

"You're so . . . matter-of-fact about all this," I observed.

"I hope I don't seem cold. I make a living putting things in places. It's the only thing I know how to do. I, um, I went to therapy once."

"Oh, really?"

Did that sound accusatory? I didn't mean it to. I've been seeing Nancy on a weekly basis for years, ever since my first anxiety attack, which came cleverly disguised as a heart attack.

"I mean, literally, just one time," he explained. "It wasn't a good fit for me because I'm not very good at talking to strangers."

"You're doing fine tonight," I said.

"That says more about you than me. The therapist told me I was thinking my feelings rather than feeling them. And that I needed to work more on feeling my feelings. But when you're raising a teenager, who has time to feel? I think you have to be a doer, not a feeler. Know what I mean?"

"Yep. In fact, sometimes I find myself thinking, 'I'll decide how I feel about that next week.' You have to put it on the calendar. And then my daughter keeps telling me I should date. *Date?* When?"

Okay, Coco has never said that. Why was I making this up?

Because it's getting late, and I have to know where I stand with this guy.

"So you don't date much?" he asked.

"Nope," I said.

I am not counting all the terrible dates I've had. Those don't even qualify as dates. And I'm not counting Chuck That. Or the sous-chef I saw a few times when I was on the rebound from Chuck That. Or any of those disastrous Match.com lunch dates. Yes, there were dozens of them, one worse than the next. But I didn't enjoy any of them—and I paid for my own damn meal every time. Those were not dates. They don't count!

"Me, neither," he said. "Have you tried online dating?"

"No!" I protested quickly. "I mean, not with any real . . . success. All the guys—er, the couple of guys I met online, were weirdos or married or religious nuts or survivalists still mad the Y2K thing didn't pan out. Or guys who lived at home with their mothers or . . . How 'bout you?"

"I tried the one called e-Symphony or e-Melody. Something like that."

"You did eHarmony?" I asked.

"Yeah, that's it."

"And?"

"It was a lot of work," he said. "It seemed too much like a job, answering all those questions. So then I tried Craigslist."

"You did not!" I said. "Isn't that where—"

"Yeah. I got lots of interesting photos and offers for sensual massages." He laughed. "I had no idea. But I did find a great old Eames chair on Craigslist. Some nice light fixtures, too.

So it wasn't a complete waste of time. To tell you the truth, the only woman I see on a regular basis is my sister, Laura. She can have visitors on weekends, so I see her then."

He is so nice.

"Is the . . . place nearby?" I asked.

"It's not bad. About two hours, each way. And then once you get to the prison, you have to stand in line for an hour. And then Laura and I visit for a few hours. It ends up being a whole day. I try to make it there every weekend, but sometimes I can't."

I wonder if they allow visitors to bring in food. I could find a darling picnic basket and fill it with fabulous treats and send it with Andrew. I could win her over. She'd like me before she even met me. Wait, listen! He's still talking.

"Webb's on a traveling soccer team. They have games most Saturdays. The only other woman I see is my lawyer, Tamra. I see her quite a bit."

Of course he was seeing somebody back home. Of course. But Tamra? Tamra, my ass. She was Tammy in high school. But a lawyer? Shit.

"Tamra and I go to lunch every couple of weeks. I like her a lot. And she looks like Glen Campbell. Or maybe Glen Campbell's sister. Tamra's pushing eighty these days. I guess that's my type. Is there a support group for men who have a thing for Glen Campbell?"

It was nothing! Thank you, God! I love lawyers! What would we do without lawyers?

"I don't know about a support group for you," I said. "But

my daughter plans to study psychology, so I'm pretty much doomed. You might as well commit me right now."

He smiled. "I have no idea what my son will study. He recently told me he wants to be a caveman."

"A what?"

"Don't ask," he said. "I think it means he doesn't want to work. He's very laid-back. I try to see that as a good thing."

"It *is* a good thing."

"Right. But when he tells me there's a college major called Leisure Studies, can you understand why I get a little nervous?"

I couldn't help laughing. He was nice. And funny. And honest.

"My daughter is so rigid and tense." I said. *Wait. Was I describing Coco or me?* "It'd be interesting to see how our kids got along."

"I'd love it," he said.

"Really?"

"Of course. I'd love my son to meet a young woman who was excited about her future."

We walked and talked about everything—until we saw a man unloading bread at a café.

I looked at my watch. It was ten minutes after five.

"We have to get back to the hotel," I said.

Andrew hailed a cab. Ten minutes later when we pulled up to the hotel, we found the bellhops eating chocolate-chip cookies.

"Can I help you with your bags?" he asked.

"No, no," I said. "I'm fine. I really have to run, though."

And with that I dashed toward the elevator, leaving Andrew in the lobby.

I cursed myself all the way up to the sixth floor and continued cursing myself as I threw my makeup bag and unworn pajamas in my suitcase. Why hadn't I given him a business card? Why couldn't I blow off the flight and take a later one?

Because I had to get back to Coco, that's why. So why didn't I tell him that, so he'd know that I was interested?

The self-critical rant played through my head as I raced back to the elevator and rode it to the lobby, where I found Andrew, waiting for me. He carried my bag to the front entrance and hailed a cab.

"Can I call you?" he asked as I climbed in the cab.

"Of course," I said. "My number in Chicago is 312—"

"No, I mean, I want to call you in Paris. Is there a number where I can reach you?"

I dug Solange's cell phone out of my purse.

"Ugh, I don't even know the number on this thing," I said. "Why don't you just call me at Solange's apartment?"

I wrote the phone number on the back of my shopping list. "Here," I said. "Coco and I will be in Paris until Saturday."

CHAPTER 41

Webb

$\mathcal{I}$ could smell the foul cheese as soon as we walked in the apartment. I didn't have time to mess around. I grabbed her bag and started for the bathroom.

"Wait!" Coco said. "That's not your bag."

"I know," I answered, rushing toward the bathroom. "But I left something in here that I need to . . . do something with."

"Webb! That's *not* your bag. It's mine. Just tell me what you want, and I'll give it to you." She was trying to pull the bag from my hand.

"Hey, hey, hey," I replied, pretending to joke around. "I'm serious. I need to get my—"

"*I'm* serious," she said, grabbing a handle of the bag. "This is *my* bag. Give it to me, and I'll give you your bag."

Oh, God. I really hated to do it, but there was no alternative. With one quick motion, I pulled the bag away from her. I was just two steps from the safety of the bathroom.

"What the hell do you think you're doing?" Coco yelled. Now she was trying to pin me against the wall.

"I put something in here I need," I said. "I'll just be a second."

She was suddenly in my face and swatting at the bag. "No! You do *not* have my permission to take my bag in the bathroom! No means no!"

"Coco," I said, holding the bag behind my back. "If you really want to know, it's something embarrassing that I don't want you to see."

"Like what?" She was still trying to grab the bag from me. Then she stopped. Her arms dropped. She smiled. "Is it a . . . condom?"

"A *what*?"

I didn't know how to play this. *Should I laugh? Should I say that it was a condom? That wasn't such a bad idea.* I turned and threw the bag in the bathroom and then locked myself in with it.

"Up, up and away, si'l vous plait," I warbled in a fake French accent from the other side of the door.

Quickly, I fished the stinky cheese out of the bag's side pocket and flung it in the toilet with a humiliating *PLONK*. I flushed and rezipped the bag.

When I emerged from the bathroom, Coco was sitting sideways on a chair in the living room. Her arms were crossed. Her legs were dangling over one arm of the chair. She looked cute as hell. She also looked mad as hell.

"Sorry about that," I said, setting the bag down gently at her feet.

Silence.

"Coco," I tried again. "You'd laugh if you knew what this was all about. I should just tell you."

"Actually, I don't even *want* to know. I just want to know what train station you're leaving from so we can figure out how to get there."

We rode the Metro in silence. When we got to the station, we ran to the platform. The doors to my train were closed.

"Pound on the doors," Coco said. "See if they'll open them for you."

I did. As if by miracle, the doors opened.

"Go!" she said. "Good-bye."

"Bye," I said. "This was . . . fun, right?"

"Yeah, right," she said.

I jumped up the trains steps with one leap and threw my bag inside the train only to realize I had no euros left. None. I'd spent everything buying time at the Internet place. The train door had closed behind me.

I hit the door panel with the palm of my hand and the door reopened. Coco was still standing on the platform.

"You, uh, don't have any euros I could borrow, do you?"

"What?" she asked.

The sound in the station—announcements, bells, trains arriving—was deafening.

"It's just that . . . I don't have any money left for water or food," I said. "And it's a long ride back to Madrid."

"Oh," she said, digging in her back pockets. She pulled out several bills. "Here. Take these."

"Thanks!" I said. "I'll pay you back. Sometime."

"Don't worry about it," she said. "Oh! I forgot to give you your shirt back."

The door was closing.

"Keep it!" I said.

But I don't think she heard me.

CHAPTER 42

Coco

$\mathcal{I}$t wasn't until the train pulled away that I realized I should've offered to split the train fare with Webb. Between that and keeping his shirt, he must've thought I was a selfish bitch.

Shit.

The problem was, once I realized he'd seen my hideous undies (which I should've thrown away *before* we left Chicago) and foam-padded pink bra (which I never should've bought in the *first* place, but once I did, I should've tossed it when I realized how stupid it was, or at least when the foam started buckling), I was sunk. And then when he insisted on taking another look at them? In the bathroom, no less? I couldn't get my mojo back.

Mom and her stupid pack-your-worst-underwear approach to life. *Brilliant, Mom.*

On the other hand, maybe he was just being honest. Maybe

he really *was* just getting rid of the condoms. Maybe he was nervous about his dad finding them, so he wanted to ditch them before he left.

But if so, why did he think it was so damn funny? Was having tantric sex with me such a hilarious impossibility? Was it really such a big freakin' *joke*?

Even if he hadn't seen my underwear and bras, he still wouldn't have wanted to have sex with me. Why had I seemed like such a brownnose and a prude? Why did I say *ick* when he mentioned condoms? And why did I laugh at his singing? Why did I make fun of his namesake, Jimmy Webb? I'd obviously hurt his feelings.

I rode the Metro back to the apartment and crawled onto the futon with my camera. I clicked through all the pictures I'd taken at the Internet café. He was adorable in every shot with his wide-open smile and rumpled hair. I, meanwhile, looked like a girl who wears granny panties and padded bras—which I *don't*. Not anymore, anyway.

I crawled under the covers and hoped to die.

Then I remembered the condoms I'd stashed in Solange's medicine cabinet. I got up and hid them in the bottom of my bag. I'd stick them in someone's locker at school when I got home.

CHAPTER 43

Andrew

When I finally climbed into bed, the digital alarm clock between Webb's bed and mine read 6:52. I needed sleep, but all I could think about was when I should call Daisy.

I knew from spending just those few hours with her that she was the kind of woman who would find the story of my note—*our* note, really—funny if I told it in the right way. Which I could. And I would.

Surely she didn't think I was a first-class ass, or she wouldn't have spent hours with me when we were both exhausted.

I needed to tell her about it for my sake, as much as hers. Secrets have no place between two people who are trying to build a relationship. And that's what I wanted to do. If this wasn't kismet, what was?

I looked at the clock again: 6:55. This was what Einstein meant when he said time was relative.

I couldn't call her before eight o'clock in the evening. But at that hour, she and her daughter might be out to dinner. So I had to call either earlier or later.

I decided I'd call in the afternoon to make sure she got back safely. Or was that too cloying? Women hated being patronized, and who could blame them?

On the other hand, she'd be tired when she arrived in Paris. She might want to nap in the afternoon. So I should call before the nap. Or after the nap?

I looked at the clock again. 6:57.

I got up, pulled on some clothes, and went downstairs in search of coffee.

CHAPTER 44

Daisy

There I was, racing by cab to catch a flight back to Paris after having been up all night with a handsome, kind, intelligent man. It felt like something on the Lifetime channel.

I pulled out a compact and checked my face, expecting to see a wrinkled old hag.

Instead, I found a woman who looked like a prettier, younger version of myself. I couldn't help grinning at the image in the mirror.

As the cab pulled into the departing flights area, I applied lipstick and pulled my hair up into a topknot—my cleaning lady hairstyle, as Coco called it.

"Merci, er, gracias," I said to the driver, handing him forty euros.

"De nada, guapa," he said as he carried my bag to the curb. Then he winked at me.

"Uh, right," I said.

I made my way through the security checkpoint and found my gate. The boarding process had already begun, so I knew I wouldn't have time to get coffee. I gazed with envy at a man holding a steaming cup of black coffee. He looked American or British. He saw me staring at his coffee.

"That's what I need," I said, smiling.

"Here," he replied. "Take it. I haven't touched it yet."

"Oh, God, no," I said, laughing. "I wouldn't dream of it."

"Are you sure?"

"Absolutely. I'll get some on the plane."

He smiled and, unless I was crazy, he subtly checked me out. *What was going on? First the cabdriver and now this? Was I giving off the I've-been-up-all-night-with-a-man vibe? Maybe so. But I hadn't slept with him, for heaven's sake. I couldn't have a sex afterglow. So why all the attention?*

Minutes after takeoff, the flight attendants began distributing lukewarm coffee and rubbery croissants. Had I not been famished and caffeine deprived, I would've passed on both. But instead, I ate and drank with pleasure until we hit a bumpy spot and I spilled coffee on my slacks.

"Shit," I murmured.

A man across the aisle smiled at me and handed me his napkin.

Okay, this was getting ridiculous. Men never looked at me anymore. Well, with the possible exception of creepy men who stuck notes in my purse. Maybe I should stay up all night more often.

I glanced through the in-flight magazine distractedly, but I couldn't muster the energy to focus. So I closed my eyes and thought about Andrew.

He was nice, wasn't he? It wasn't just my imagination. He was kind and smart and arty. And he was honest. And, my God, the story about his sister. How generous of him to adopt her baby.

I drifted off, dreamily, thinking of Andrew and his son.

When we landed, I went straight to the airport exit and found the waiting line of cabs.

"Montmartre," I said, climbing in the first available taxi.

A half hour later I was walking in the door of Solange's apartment. Poor Coco was cocooned in her futon, right where I'd left her. Nestled in a blanket, she looked like a tragic ballerina in *Swan Lake*.

"Sweet baby girl," I said, kissing her awake. "Are you feeling better?"

"No," she said, sniffling. "A million times worse."

I put my hand to her forehead. She felt cool to the touch. I kissed her again. Her cheeks tasted salty.

"Can I make you some toast?" I asked. "Or hot tea?"

"No." She sighed, covering her eyes. "I need to take a shower."

She crawled out from under her covers. She was wearing her favorite flannel pajamas.

"Your jammies," I said. "Did your bag finally arrive?"

"Huh?" Coco said, looking down at herself. "Oh, yeah. Someone, uh, delivered it here yesterday."

"That's great, honey," I said. "I bet it was the stress of not having your things that made you feel sick."

Coco turned and gave me a glacial stare. "No, that's *not* what it was. So can we just *drop* it?"

Oh, God. Here we go again.

"And it probably means I won't even get the freakin' five hundred *dollars*," she said, schlepping toward the bathroom.

She was slamming the bathroom door behind her just as the phone rang.

"I'm sure we can still get you that money," I yelled toward her. And then, without thinking clearly, I picked up the ringing phone.

"Hello?" I said.

"Hi, it's me, Andrew. Is it okay for me to call and make sure you got back okay?"

CHAPTER 45

Webb

"Where have you *been*?" Dad boomed when I finally got back to the hotel. It was almost eight thirty that night.

"I had to, uh, go get my bag," I said.

He looked at the black duffel I was carrying. "Oh. Is that yours?"

"Yeah," I confirmed, sitting on the bed. "Finally, huh?"

I was hungry, thirsty, tired, and stiff from the long train ride. Plus, a low-grade depression was setting in—a result of my lackluster performance with Coco. Dad, on the other hand, seemed weirdly energetic. I hoped it wasn't fueled by his anger at me.

"So?" Dad said. "What'd you think?"

"About . . . ?"

"The show. Last night."

"Oh, right," I said. "Right, right, right. It was . . . cool. It looked . . . *great.*"

"I'm glad you liked it," Dad said, smiling. He sure seemed to be in a good mood. "I thought all that digital stuff would appeal to you."

"Uh-huh," I said. I felt like a complete jerk for missing Dad's big night. "I'd like to see it again. Tomorrow maybe?"

"Let's do that," he said. "We should go to the Prado, too. I know we went there last time we were here, but it's worth another visit."

"Okay."

"And I haven't had my fill of tapas yet," Dad continued. "Have you?"

"No, I'm starving."

"Then let's go get some dinner," Dad said, mussing up my hair. "Good job getting your bag, Webb. I was afraid that thing was a goner."

"Yeah," I said. "Me, too."

We walked to a narrow street called Cava Baja and ate appetizers off little plates. Dad was digging the squid and octopus. My favorite was tortilla Española, which isn't a tortilla at all, but more like a cold potato omelet, which sounds worse than squid, but it's really good. Dad ordered beers for both of us.

"I wish we had the same approach to drinking that Europeans have," Dad said. "Kids here grow up drinking with their families. Not a lot. Just a little. So then when they go off to college, drinking doesn't occupy such a huge role, like it does back home."

"Uh-huh," I said, trying to force the beer down. It tasted like dirty socks and reminded me of stinky cheese.

"The stories you hear of binge drinking on college campuses," Dad continued, shaking his head. "And alcohol poisoning. Moderation might sound boring, Webb, but it can save your life."

"Yeah," I said, remembering with horror the sound of the cheese dropping into the toilet. No wonder Coco looked suicidal when I emerged from the bathroom. Or did she look homicidal? I could tell she wanted to kill somebody. Most likely me.

When we got back to the hotel, Dad put his arm around my shoulder. "Let me guess," he said. "You want to duck into the business center one last time tonight."

"That's okay," I said.

"No, no," Dad said, all jokey and nice. "Go ahead. I've got to make a phone call, anyway. Somewhat personal. I'll see you upstairs."

I retreated to the business center and logged on. I had no new messages, so I started writing one.

Fr: Webbn@com
To: CocoChi@com
Subject: Strangers on a Train Platform—After-Action Report

Hey there, Blouse Girl. Just wanted to say thanks for letting me visit.

I hope I didn't do irreparable harm to your psyche with my singing.

One complaint: You didn't tell me how pretty you are.
That was a nice surprise. Thanks for spotting me 20
euros for the trip home. I'll pay you back with interest
when we

I stopped. When we *what*? Saw each other again? She wouldn't want to see me again. When we got back home? She might not want to give me her home address. I remembered the way she looked at me when she was trying to tear her bag out of my arms. When we . . .

Nothing.

I deleted the message without sending it and went upstairs to bed.

CHAPTER 46

Coco

$\mathscr{I}$t was Mom's idea to spend the afternoon at the Louvre. I was glad to go because at least if we were looking at paintings, we wouldn't have to talk to each other. I was in one of those moods where everything Mom said seemed like a criticism of me, which made me respond in some bratty-assed way, and so on and so on, ad nauseam.

Let's face it. The let's-all-pack-our-worst-underwear-so-the-only-guy-I've-ever-been-even-mildly-interested-in-will-see-my-crappy-undies thing was *her* idea. And maybe she didn't mean to ruin my life. But that wasn't the point. She *did* ruin it, whether she meant to or not. And to be perfectly honest, I wasn't sure she *didn't* want to ruin my life and keep me from having a boyfriend. Just because she hated men on account of one guy who didn't practice safe sex and got her preggers in Paris didn't mean that *I* never wanted to have sex. If I thought about it too much, I would completely lash out at her, and that wouldn't be good for either of us.

So I was fine with her idea of going to the Louvre. I thought maybe looking at art might help me get my mind off the disaster with Webb.

But it was just the opposite.

When we got back to Solange's apartment, I told Mom I wanted to check e-mail while she made dinner. Of course Webb hadn't written to me. (Why *would* he?) But I had something I needed to tell him.

Fr: CocoChi@com
To: Webbn@com
Subject: How life imitates art and vice versa

Hi Webb. If I'm tired, you must be wiped out. I hope you didn't fall asleep on the train and wake up in Italy. I also hope you can forgive me for not offering to give you more money. I totally should've paid for half of your train fare. I know those tickets weren't cheap. And it was so great of you to make the trip to see little old me. :)

Oh brother. I deleted that last sentence and started a new paragraph.

My mom and I spent the afternoon at the Louvre. I was too tired to see straight, but Mom really wanted to go. I'm glad we did because there was one painting that looked exactly like how I felt the whole time we (meaning you and I) were together. The painting is by Jean-Antoine Watteau. It's called *Pierrot*. It's a picture of a guy wearing a ridiculous white clown costume. Or maybe it's a bunny suit. I'm not sure, but anyway, it's a ridiculous costume made even worse by a pair of silly, floppy, ribbon-tied shoes. The guy looks like he might've been smiling earlier, but now the smile is gone and he's left standing there, looking and feeling ridiculous, like he's in a play and he just realized he's forgotten his lines. Or, like he's at a party, and he thought it was a costume party so he suited up in this weird-ass costume only to realize it's not a costume party. And now all he can do is just stand there like an idiot dressed in a rabbit suit.

I think the reason this painting stopped me in my tracks is because that's exactly how I felt with you: like a freakin' clown. I couldn't string a noun and a verb together to save my life. I just felt like the worst and bitchiest version of myself. Does that make any sense at all?

I reread the message. No, it didn't make any sense at all. I deleted it without sending and went back to the apartment.

CHAPTER 47

Andrew

I couldn't help it. I called Daisy again that night after we got back from dinner.

"I realize I'm violating every rule of courtship known to man by calling you a second time today, but I have to read you the review of the show in today's *El País*," I began.

"I'm dying to hear it," she said.

I could hear some commotion in the background. "Am I interrupting something?" I asked.

"No, no," she said. "I'm just making dinner."

"I can call back later."

"No need," she said. "I can cook and talk. Read me the review, please."

"Okay," I said, then cleared my throat dramatically. "*Love in the Postdigital Age* opened last night at the Crystal Palace in Retiro Park—"

"Wait," she interrupted. "Why is this review written in English if it's in a Spanish newspaper?"

"I had it translated by someone here at the hotel," I said. "May I continue?"

"Please do."

I cleared my throat again. "The exhibit, intended to showcase how modern technology has changed the art of romance, does so through an array of interactive artwork that employs late twentieth- and early twenty-first-century gadgetry. Farewell to love letters inked on parchment paper. Hello, love text messages, e-mails, and cell phone serenades. In all, more than a hundred computer monitors—many modeled to look like human faces—combine to demonstrate how technology is reshaping the concept of love. Among the highlights of the show is *Spin the Cell Phone,* an interactive piece by Canadian artist/gamer Tad Nordent who invites viewers to 'play' his exhibit much as young lovers now play the dating field. Also of note is *PorNOgraphy* by Juan Tomás Alvarez, which juxtaposes images of the artist's life partner alongside pornographic pictures of unknown women that attempt, through clever digital effects, to erode the image of the beloved."

I heard something crash on the other end of the line. "Are you still there?" I asked.

"Sorry," Daisy said. "I dropped a pan. But I'm glad someone explained that pornography thing to me. I didn't get it. Keep reading, please."

"Okay, I'm going to skim some of this, including the bit about the 'impressive exhibit design.'"

"No, read it," she insisted.

"No, no. This is the part I want you to hear. 'Underscoring the theme of love's altered state in our postmodern world were the trays of warm cookies and buttery tarts served to guests, who couldn't help but feel—' "

"You're making this up," she said, giggling.

"I'm not," I reported. "Listen. 'One couldn't help but feel a certain wistfulness for a simpler age when people had time to bake, and when romance could begin with something as humble as paper, pen, and a postage stamp. A postage *what*?' "

"Is that really what it says?"

"I never lie about reviews," I assured her. "And something else. Remember those protesters we saw when we were leaving the park?"

"Yeah. What was that about?"

"Listen to this," I said. "It's a sidebar to the story. 'Cinco por Cinco, a small but increasingly visible group of Amish extremists—"

"Amish extremists? Isn't that a contradiction in terms?"

"I'm not so sure," I said. "We have lots of Amish in Missouri. They're pretty extreme. No electricity. No insurance. No marrying or socializing outside their community."

"Different strokes for different folks," she said. "Keep reading."

"Cinco por Cinco, a small but increasingly visible group of Amish extremists, has vowed to demonstrate in front of Retiro Park while the exhibit is in place. The members of Cinco por Cinco believe the Internet is Satan's toy and that it represents the single biggest threat to faithful love. The stated goal of the group is to rid the world of electronic communication, beginning with the Internet, and return to a simpler predigital era, where hands were used to sew, quilt, cook, farm, and pray. The group has threatened to use low-tech terrorist means to achieve their goals. Until then, the members vow to fast on water and uncooked rolled oats."

"Oh, for God's sake," she said. "They're freaks. It's a cult, isn't it? Full of people who can't think for themselves and—"

She paused. I knew she was remembering my sister.

"It's okay," I said. "I just thought you'd be interested to hear that."

"Yes, thank you. So how are you?"

"Fine. Did you get any sleep today?" I asked.

"A little on the plane," she said. "My daughter was in one of her moods. So we spent the day at the Louvre. At least we wouldn't have to talk to each other." She laughed. "See what a great parent I am?"

"I forced my son to drink a beer at dinner tonight," I admitted. "And it was the worst beer I've ever had in my life. It tasted like dirty socks."

She laughed harder. I could hear whatever she was cooking sizzling in the pan. I wished I were right there. I wished we were face-to-face.

"There should be awards for parents like us," she said. "I mean, really. Leaving a sick child alone in a foreign country? Some mama grizzly I am."

"Well, I lost my son for most of the day," I confessed. "I had no idea where he was. For hours."

"Do you realize," she replied, "that our children are the ones who'll decide what nursing homes we go to? They'll be our caregivers. Our guardians. How terrifying is that?"

"Very. Would it be annoying if I called you again tomorrow?" I asked.

"Terribly annoying," she said.

"Hmm. I just might have to risk it."

"You better," she said.

"I'm glad you gave me your phone number."

I was saying anything just to keep her on the line. It had been years since I'd felt like this. I needed to hear her voice to believe she was real.

"I'm glad you asked," she said softly. Then her voice rose. "Oh, wait! I have to tell you something funny. That line in the review about romance beginning with something as humble as paper and pen? Get this. On the flight from Chicago, some creep wrote me a secret admirer note and stuck it in my purse when I wasn't looking. How do you like *that*? And here's the kicker. The guy was traveling with his wife or girlfriend."

CHAPTER 48

Daisy

I was too critical. I could hear it in Andrew's voice.

"How do you know the guy was married?" he asked. "Or that he had a girlfriend?"

"I forget," I said, immediately regretting having told him. "It was something he wrote in the note about not traveling alone."

"That could mean a lot of things," Andrew said quickly.

Why was he defending the guy? Was it to make the point that I was too quick to criticize? He didn't know me well enough to point out my character flaws.

Breathe, Nancy would say. *Stop thinking like this. Stop taking it personally. Are you angry at him? No. Your parents? No. Then who are you angry with?* Nobody!

Breathe.

Solange's cell phone started ringing.

"Oops, I need to go," I said. "Can we talk another time?"

"Sure," he said. "Good-bye."

I had to dump out the contents of my purse to find Solange's cell phone. "Hello?" I said on the fifth chirp.

"Hello yourself," Solange said. "Am I waking you?"

"For your information," I said, "I haven't been to sleep since I saw you."

Solange insisted on hearing a tick-tock of my entire evening and morning with Andrew.

"Very nice," she said when I finished. "Can I tell you what Andrew's reputation is in the small world of European museum curators?"

"Oh, God," I moaned. "That bad?"

"He is the nicest man on earth," Solange stated. "Several years ago when I first thought about hiring him to design a show for me, I checked his references. I could not find one person who had even a so-so comment about him. Everyone adores Andrew—from board members to executive directors to custodians. He does excellent work and has no ego. A masterpiece of a man."

I smiled to myself. *I was right. He was nice.*

"So why isn't he married?" I asked.

"I could ask the same of you," Solange said. "Maybe because you are both workaholics. Or single parents. Or because you waste your time on . . . what was that idiot's name? Dick?"

"Chuck," I said. "But never mind him. Does Andrew pick up women at every show, like he did me?"

"You seemed to enjoy it," Solange said. "But I am not

calling to talk about you. Or Andrew. I am wondering about Coco. Is she feeling better?"

"Yes and no," I said. "Physically she's fine. I think it was just jet lag. But she's in a mood. Something must be going on back home. She's down at that Internet place again right now."

"Let her use my cell phone," Solange said. "It has Internet capabilities. She can e-mail her friends from the apartment."

"Are you sure?"

"Of course I am sure. And then take the phone back to Chicago with you. Save it for your next trip here. Phones are inexpensive in Europe. It is not like the States. Here we buy cheap phones and then use phone cards."

As Solange spoke, Coco was letting herself in the apartment.

"Here," I said, handing the phone to Coco. "Someone wants to say hello."

I watched Coco talk on the phone. Her eyes looked tired. Sadder. Older. Something was definitely bothering her, but I didn't dare ask without risking another meltdown.

While she talked to Solange, I lit candles in the living room and finished preparing our dinner: ratatouille crepes, flash-fried spinach, rocket greens salad, and half a baguette.

"Would you like a small glass of wine with dinner?" I asked Coco when she was off the phone. "There's a bottle in the fridge that Solange left for us."

"Mom, you know I don't drink."

"I know and I'm glad. But since you're going off to college in the fall where students have been known to drink, I thought you might want a little taste of—"

"I *said* I don't want any," she snarled. Her moral smugness felt like a slap in the face.

"That's fine," I said. I poured myself a glass of wine, ate my dinner, and thought about Andrew.

He called for the third time at almost midnight. I took the phone back to the bedroom with me.

"I know it's the height of rudeness to call this late," he said. "But I have to tell you something, and you're going to think I'm a complete idiot when you hear this."

Oh God, here it comes. He's married. Or he's seeing someone else. Or he's gay. Or he has herpes.

"Go on," I said, closing the bedroom door and bracing for the worst. My chest was already tight. I felt a familiar anger rise up inside me.

"You know when we were talking earlier?" he said.

"Uh-huh." I put my free hand on my heart to remind it to keep beating.

He paused. I could hear him breathing heavily. "About romance and . . . handwritten love notes and . . ." He paused again.

"Yes?" I said crisply. I hated my tone, but I could feel myself pulling away from him just by the hint of what was coming. I was an expert at walking away from things. People. Jobs. From any situation, really. I was already leaving him in my mind.

"Um, well, I wanted to, er, explain . . ." He was stumbling.

"Look," I said, forcing myself to fake a smile so I didn't sound as angry as I felt. "We don't have to do this. It was great meeting you and spending the evening together, but it doesn't have to be anything more than that." I manufactured a light laugh. "You don't have to *break up* with me, for God's sake. We were never even together."

"No," he said. "Wait. Stop. I'm terrible at this."

"Then just *tell* me what's on your mind," I snapped. "Top of mind, as the therapists say."

"Okay then," he said softly. "You. You're on my mind. That's what I wanted to tell you."

"*Seriously?*" I felt my whole body relax.

"Yes," he said. "And not only that, you're gentle on my mind, too. Wait—is that too corny to say?"

"No." I couldn't help smiling, and this time it was real. My chest muscles relaxed. "So do you have to pay Jimmy Webb a royalty every time you filch one of his lines?"

Now it was his turn to laugh. "That's a John Hartford song. And he's dead."

"Oh," I said. "Too bad."

"He was a St. Louis boy," he said. "If ever you come to town, I'll show you Hartford's star on the St. Louis Walk of Fame."

"Maybe I'll do that sometime."

"I hope you will," he said. "Good night, Daisy."

"Good night, Andrew."

Day 5: Thursday

Musée Rodin
Entrée Musée
Plein Tarif
6,00

Musée Rodin
Entrée Musée
Plein Tarif
6,00

www.musee-rodin.fr

Musée Rodin
plan

MUSEO NACIONAL DEL PRADO
Plano
Primavera

MUSEO NACIONAL DEL PRADO

N° del Prado s/n. 28014 Madrid
www.museoprado.es
Teléfono +34 902 10 70 77

Sala 10A
GRECO
La Trinidad

Sala 26
RIBERA
El sueño de

Sala
ZURBARÁN

Sala 12
VELÁZQUEZ
Las lanzas

Sala 12
VELÁZQUEZ
El bufón don Diego
de Acedo 'el Primo'

Sala 12
VELÁZQUEZ
Las meninas

Sala 28
MURILLO

Sala 29
MURILLO
La inmaculada
concepción de

Ground floor

Room 3 | Room 4 | Room 5 | Room 6 | Room 7
Room 8
Room 8 bis
Room 1 | Room 2

Bored Pretty Glaze Knickknacks

(ARMISTICE?)

museum entrance :
presentation of
Biron

Room 5 : *The Walking Man*
12 *The Cathedral*
13 *Interior decoration*

First floor

Room 12 | Room 13 | Room 14 | Room 15 | Room
Room 10 | Room 9
Room 11

Upstairs landing
22 Cast iron technique

Room 13 :
Male portraits and painting
Van Gogh, Renoir, Mone

CHAPTER 49

Webb

I slept till noon. I thought Dad would be pissed, but he wasn't.

"Hey, buddy," he said when I found him downstairs in the hotel restaurant. He was drinking coffee and reading the *International Herald Tribune*. "Sleep okay?"

"Yeah," I said.

"Great," he answered, folding the paper. "Do you want to get something to eat here, or shall we get out in the real world?"

"I don't care."

"You don't care?" he asked. He was smiling with his mouth, but frowning with his eyebrows. "You *have* to care. That's your job in life: to care about something. Or someone. That's even better."

He was sure in a banner mood.

"Let's walk over to the Plaza Mayor," Dad said.

"Okay."

"And then we'll hit the Prado," Dad continued. "I'd like to see the Velázquez paintings. And you like the ones by Hieronymus Bosch, remember?"

"Yeah," I said.

"And then I thought, if you still wanted to, we could take another look at the postdigital show together," Dad said. "I'd really like to hear your thoughts on the exhibit, especially the gaming installations."

Gaming installations? What the hell was he talking about?

"Okay," I said, nodding.

"And then," Dad said, standing up from the table, "we'll find a great place to have dinner. Maybe hear some music? That sound okay to you?"

"Sure," I said. *Fine. Whatever.* I didn't care one way or the other what we did.

"This'll be great," Dad said. "So why don't you make a stop at the business center before we head out for the day, and then we'll—"

"Not necessary," I said.

Dad looked at me like I'd sprouted a second head. "What's wrong?"

"Nothing," I said with the certainty that comes with defeat. "There's just . . . nothing there for me."

CHAPTER 50

Coco

Mom decided we should spend Thursday afternoon at the Rodin Museum.

"You'll love this place," she told me, all jolly and smiley, as we walked to the Metro. "It's in a lovely old mansion where lots of nineteenth- and twentieth-century artists rented space to live and work."

Who cared? Not me. I couldn't wait to get back to Chicago. The trip had been such a disaster. It was actually my worst vacation ever.

I studied the people on the Metro. Two college-age girls in scarves were talking and laughing about something. *Annoying.* A woman was holding hands with a young boy who had green snot dripping from his nose. *Disgusting.* A couple of professional-looking men were on their way to work. One guy seemed to be checking out Mom. *One hundred percent gross!*

I hated Paris. The smug people. The fussy food. The stinky

Metro with its B.O.-y smells. And once we got to the Rodin Museum, I hated that, too.

"You'll enjoy this," Mom said, handing me a study guide to all the sculptures.

Well, I didn't. And for the record, the sculpture I hated most was called *The Kiss*. It was a marble sculpture of a naked man and woman right as they're about to kiss. I didn't hate it because it made me think about Webb. We really didn't kiss at all, other than the two little cheek pecks he gave me when we met at the train station. Those weren't real kisses. It was just a corny greeting. And he didn't kiss me *once* after that. So basically his desire for me evaporated, beginning the moment we met face-to-face.

The more I stared at *The Kiss,* the more I thought about Webb. The guy in Rodin's sculpture is totally zoned out, like he's about to kiss the woman, but he doesn't want to. He'd rather be reading his book. I hated *The Kiss* and people who kissed and everything about kissing.

I even hated Rodin. I couldn't believe the museum included sculptures by Camille Claudel. She was Rodin's student and mistress, which just goes to prove that pervy teachers have been around forever. Actually, her work was pretty good. But Rodin apparently dumped her when she started going crazy. Her family eventually committed her to an insane asylum where she lived for decades before dying alone. *Quelle* charming.

The only thing I liked in the whole museum was a sculpture I found outside in the garden. It was called *Balzac* and was this huge creepy sculpture of some famously cranky writer

I'd never heard of. According to the guide, when Rodin unveiled the sculpture in 1898, Parisians booed it. But I liked it. I especially liked Balzac's sinister-looking Dracula cape and his crazy I-don't-give-a-rat's-ass-what-people-think-of-me expression. He looked like how I felt.

I sat in the grass staring at Mr. Balzac and wondering how long it'd be before my mom tried to commit me to an insane asylum. It would be completely typical of her, but also completely unfair. At least Camille Claudel got to have sex before she went to the loony bin and died.

Dr. Guillotin was right. A sharp blade to the neck could be an act of mercy.

CHAPTER 51

Andrew

Webb and I were back at the Crystal Palace when I felt my BlackBerry vibrate.

"I'm going to take this outside," I told Webb. "I'll meet you back in here."

"Okay," he said neutrally. He seemed bored by the show. Maybe seeing it once had been enough. I couldn't disagree with him.

The call was from Solange.

"If you're going to tell me there's a problem with the exhibit," I said, "I won't believe you because I'm here now, and everything's perfect."

"Of course it is perfect," she said. "Thanks to you. I am calling about something else. Something more important." She sounded serious. "Daisy."

I stopped breathing. "Is something wrong?"

"Wrong?" she said. "Just the opposite. You two are more *right* for each other than any couple I've ever seen in my life."

I exhaled. "She seems great."

"No, Andrew," Solange corrected. "She does not *seem* great. She *is* great. Have you Googled her? Do you know what a *star* she is in Chicago? Wherever she works becomes the hottest restaurant in the city. She has the golden touch. She is incredible. Do you know how incredible she is?"

"I'm learning," I said.

"Listen to me," Solange pressed on. "Daisy has not shown this much interest in a man for years. I do not know what you said or did to her, and I do not want to know. But whatever it is, she is interested. And if you are interested—which you would have to be crazy *not* to be—you must act quickly. She rarely takes time off work. But she left her job last week and—"

"Yes, she told me about that—" I started to say.

"What she did *not* tell you is that she will have offers from ten restaurants waiting for her when she gets back to Chicago. And then she will throw herself into a new job, and work eighty hours a week, and—*pouf*—you will have missed your chance."

"Are you saying I should—"

"What I am *saying*," she said, as if speaking to a child, "is that if you want her, you must see her before she leaves Paris."

"But I think she's leaving Saturday. And I'm in Madrid till then."

"I am not telling you how to do it," Solange said impatiently. "I am just telling you what must be done."

"Yes, boss," I said, smiling. "Hey, I wanted to ask you about something. Did you know there were protesters on opening night?"

"Don't get me started on that. When I found out about them, I tried to arrange a meeting with their leader—Abraham or Moses or Ezekiel. I was going to offer to curate a quilt show for them for free if they would promise *not* to make a scene at my show. I was prepared to create a website, a Facebook page, some YouTube videos of their women making quilts. Of course it is the women who do all the work. This is always the way in misogynist organizations."

"So what happened?"

"They would not even speak to me," she said. "Beasts, all of them. Now, you will call Daisy, yes?"

"Right. Can you give me any suggestions on how I should—"

But the CALL ENDED message told me Solange's work was done.

CHAPTER 52

Daisy

Coco and I had dinner reservations at Petrelle, my favorite restaurant in Paris. Just walking in the door and seeing those wide-plank wooden floors and the tables—ten farm tables covered with starched white linens and piles of books—made me happy. If the Rodin Museum couldn't cheer up Coco, surely Petrelle could.

I ordered for both of us: smoked duck breast salad followed by ravioli stuffed with crayfish. As usual, every bite was perfection: confirmation that cooking was an art equal to any other. Food was as important as love. The body needed it. And the quality of food, like the quality of love, mattered.

"Coco, look," I said, chewing. "Do you see the cat under that table? That's what I love about this place. Don't you feel like you're eating in your very own French country house?"

Coco grunted an inaudible response. I refused to let her rotten mood ruin my meal.

"Should we pick up some postcards to send Grammy and Grampa?" I asked. "And your friends back home?"

"No," she said. "Not postcards. But I need *something* to take back to my friends."

"Okay, let's think," I said, happy for any semblance of a dinner conversation. "We could get some chocolate and maybe jars of French sea salt. It's the best salt in the world. Everyone loves—"

"Mom," Coco growled, "my friends do not want *salt*."

"Right," I said.

An hour later when Coco was eating dessert and I was sipping an espresso, I had an idea. "Let's take a walk up to Sacré Coeur," I said. "The view is absolutely lovely at night."

"Everything's *lovely* to you, isn't it?" Coco said, stabbing her spoon savagely into a ramekin of flan.

I took a deep breath and counted to five. Then I reached across the table and put my hand on hers.

"Coco," I said softly. "I know something's bothering you. And I know *you* know that I am always here to listen to anything you want to talk about. But I can't read your mind. If you don't want to tell me what's wrong, that's your decision. But I won't put up with this attitude of yours. Not for one minute more."

She attacked another spoonful of flan, but her mouth began to quiver. I hated to make her cry. On the other hand, I didn't hate it enough to back down.

"I brought you here to Paris," I continued, "because I wanted you to experience this city, this *magical* city, as an adult for the first time with someone who will always love you."

Now her eyes were getting moist. Well? It was true. I did want her to see Paris as an adult with me first. I'd stolen the idea from an article I read in *People* magazine. Gwyneth Paltrow's father took her to Paris when she was young for the very same reason. Better to fall in love with Paris in the company of a parent than come here in a few years and confuse a love of Paris with love for some bozo with a sexy accent. No need for both of us to make that mistake.

"And you know," I went on, "the crazy thing about love is that you can tell the other person anything in the world, and they'll love you. No matter what."

Now she was really crying. Something was definitely up. But still, she said nothing.

"So," I said, stroking her hand, "is there something you want to talk about? I promise I won't get mad." I paused and smiled. "Or if I do, it won't last forever."

Tears were rolling down her cheeks. "No. There's nothing you can do. I'm just . . ."

"What?" I asked. "What would make you happy right now? What could we do that would make you feel happy?"

She shook her head and cried. "I don't know what I want. Just . . . nothing."

That's my girl. Like mother, like daughter.

We took a cab back to the apartment. At least she let me put my arm around her shoulder in the backseat of the car.

"Hey, I know something that'll cheer you up," I said, pulling Solange's cell phone from my purse. "Solange lent us this. You can check your e-mail on it and send texts or whatever you want to do."

I handed the phone to Coco, but she pushed it away and buried her head in her hands.

"I never want to get online again," she sobbed. "Ever!"

I closed my eyes for the rest of the cab ride.

The phone was ringing when I unlocked the apartment. "Hello?" I said hopefully.

"Hi, it's me, Andrew."

I liked that he didn't assume I'd recognize his voice, even though I did instantly.

"Hey there," I said, carrying the phone into the bedroom.

"Do you have a minute to listen to a crazy idea?" He sounded nervous.

"I do," I said.

"Okay, here goes. What would you think about meeting in Barcelona for dinner tomorrow night? With our guardians?"

"Our *what*?" I said.

"Our kids. Webb and Coco."

Day 6: Friday

Carte d'embarquement / Boarding pass
TKNE
DAISY M. SPRINKLE
PARIS - ORY
BARCELONA - BCN
1230 Y 22APR 12:05PM
1:50PM M10C MNO
VOY
AIR FRANCE

Carte d'embarquement / Boarding pass
ANDREW R. NELSON
MADRID - MAD
BARCELONA - BCN
7555 Y 22APR 1:50PM
1:40PM M 20A MNO
Spanair

Carte d'embarquement / Boarding pass
TKNE
COCO L. SPRINKLE
PARIS - ORY
BARCELONA - BCN
1230 Y 22APR 12:05PM
1:50PM M10B MNO
VOYAGEUR 026
AIR FRANCE

Carte d'embarquement / Boarding pass
WEBB G. NELSON
MADRID - MAD
BARCELONA - BCN
7555 Y 22APR 1:50PM
1:40PM M 20B MNO
Spanair

Dear Ms. 6B,

Please forgive my clumsiness while boarding. I would be more than happy to pay for the cleaning or replacement of your blouse. Truth is, I would be even happier if you'd let me take you to dinner sometime when we return to our side of the pond. That is, if you do plan to return to the U.S. (For all I know, you could be Parisian. You have That Look.)

CHAPTER 53

Webb

D ad was explaining as he packed.

"It's only an hour flight," he said. "And it is one of your favorite cities."

He was right. I liked Barcelona a lot. It was the first European city I ever visited. Dad took me there when I was seven. It's where he told me about my mom.

"And as long as we're so close," Dad went on, "it just makes sense. I don't know why I didn't think of it before we left home." He turned to look at me. "So get up and start packing, okay? Oh, and wear that nice blue jacket."

"Why?"

"Because I'd like to go somewhere nice for dinner."

"Okay. Will we have time to do Gaudí stuff?" I asked.

"Sure. Our flight leaves at one fifty. We'll be in Barcelona by three."

"Cool."

Maybe this was what I needed to shake off the Coco dust. I was still stinging from that whole thing.

"We're meeting a friend of mine for dinner," Dad added. "She has a daughter about your age. I think she'll be joining us, too."

"Serious?"

"Yeah," said Dad. "Is that okay?"

"Yeah," I said. "In fact, that'd be . . . really cool."

This was *exactly* what I needed. Something—or better yet, someone—to take my mind off Coco.

CHAPTER 54

Coco

*B*arcelona?" I asked.

Was the universe trying to torture me with all these reminders of Webb?

"It's only an hour-and-a-half flight," Mom said.

"But we're in *Paris,*" I objected. "Why do you want to keep leaving?"

And then it hit me: Mom was going through a weird emotional backdraft. I knew the whole story about her falling in love during culinary school with the master chef, my dad. Being back here with me must be churning up all kinds of crappy memories for her.

"It's not that I want to keep leaving," Mom said, carefully folding her new silk blouses in her suitcase. "But I thought we could come back when Solange is around. Wouldn't it be fun to spend time with her?"

"I guess," I said. "But this place is way too small for three people."

"It'd be fun," Mom said. "Like a slumber party."

Yeah, right.

"Maybe we'll come back next year," Mom said. "Or for Christmas. Oh, and take something nice to wear tonight. We're meeting a friend of mine for dinner."

"Fine."

"He might bring his son along," she added, on her way to the bathroom. "He's about your age."

"Does he speak English?"

"Yes," she answered from the bathroom. "It'll be fun."

Whatever.

"I'm going across the street to pick up some pastries for breakfast," I said, walking out the door. "I'll be back in five."

CHAPTER 55

Andrew

I'd conveniently forgotten to tell Daisy where I'd booked our hotel rooms.

"I'm sorry to keep calling," I said when I called to give her the hotel address.

"No, no. It's not a problem. Are you at the airport?"

"Not yet. Webb and I are waiting for a cab."

"I'm still packing," she said. "Coco's across the street picking up some breakfast for us."

"Did you tell her—" I began, turning away from Webb for privacy.

"I just said you had a son about her age," she said. "What about you?"

"Same here." I couldn't go into much detail because Webb was standing six feet away.

"This is like the grown-up version of *The Parent Trap*," she said, laughing.

"I'm not sure what you mean."

"Didn't you ever see *The Parent Trap* with Hayley Mills?" she asked. "Or the remake with Lindsay Lohan? It's the story of twin girls scheming to reunite their estranged parents."

"You're not suggesting that your daughter and my—"

"No, no. It's just the idea that you think your son needs to meet a girl like my daughter, and I think my daughter would benefit from meeting your son."

"You and Solange have a lot in common."

She laughed. "We'll meet you at nine o'clock at the restaurant you told me about, okay?"

"More than okay," I said. "See you soon."

"Bye," she said in a soft voice.

She hung up. I stayed on the line, not believing my good luck.

CHAPTER 56

Daisy

Coco was sitting on the futon, pulling apart a croissant. She refused to put it on a plate as I'd asked her to do repeatedly. Pastry crumbs were falling everywhere. She was still sulking, but I refused to let it get under my skin.

"You can leave your bag here," I said. "We'll put everything we need in my suitcase."

"Whatever," she said, sulkily stuffing the last third of the croissant in her mouth.

I counted to ten before responding. "Honey, why don't you pack your peasant blouse? You look so cute in that."

"Actually, I don't want to look *cute*," she said. "Plus it's all wrinkled." She pulled it out of her bag and made a face. "I *hate* wrinkles."

"It's supposed to be wrinkled," I said firmly. "We can iron it when we get to the hotel in Barcelona."

She tossed the blouse in my direction. I caught it and stuffed it in my suitcase next to the black pants I'd picked out for her at Galeries Lafayette.

"Do you have your toothbrush?" I asked. "Hair stuff? Makeup?"

She flounced into the bathroom.

Why did everything have to be such a struggle? I was so tired of this. Living with a teenage girl was like being sent to the gulag for seven years.

"Here," she said, handing me her wet toothbrush while rolling her eyes.

"Thank you," I said, only slightly my gritting teeth. "Don't you want to take your hair stuff or lip gloss or—"

"If I *wanted* to take it, I would've given it to you. Can we just *go* already?"

CHAPTER 57

Webb

S o first you name me after a guy who writes dopey songs. And then for my middle name, you pick a guy who lived in a church? Way to go, Dad."

Dad rubbed my hair. We were exploring the Sagrada Família, the most famous church in Barcelona.

"Jimmy Webb wrote brilliant songs," Dad said. "You'll appreciate them more when you get older. As for Antoni Gaudí, yes, he lived in the Sagrada Família when he was working on it."

"So he was basically homeless?"

"He was obsessed with his work," Dad said.

"And you think that's a good thing, don't you?"

"I guess I do," Dad admitted. "I admire artists who fall in love with their work. There's something noble about an obsession if it leads to something like this. Webb, look around. The guy was a genius. An absolute original."

He had a point. Being inside the candlelit church was like being inside a whale—except that everywhere you looked were scenes embedded in concrete honeycomb.

We'd spent the late afternoon visiting our favorite Gaudí sites: Casa Batlló, Parc Güell, and the little cottage Gaudí built for himself within the park. We saved the Sagrada Família for last. Dad rarely made me go to church at home. But places like this, he said, had spiritual lessons to teach. Sometimes I almost understood what he was talking about.

Being in the Sagrada Família made me feel absolved of the whole Coco thing. I felt like maybe I could be forgiven for lying to Dad about going to Paris. It had been such a disaster. Wasn't that penance enough?

Dad and I found a pew in the center of the church and sat down.

"I think I sorta get what this place is trying to say," I said, looking up.

"Tell me," he said.

"It's hard to put into words."

We sat in silence. There was a holy smell in the church. It would've been the perfect time and place to tell Dad about my trip to Paris. But I couldn't.

"I'll tell you what this place says to me," Dad said slowly. "It says, look what somebody can do when he's focused. When he's not multitasking."

"*Daaad,*" I groaned. "No life lessons, please."

He continued, undeterred. "It says to me, here's a man who put himself out there and wasn't afraid to look ridiculous."

I thought about how ridiculous I'd looked with Coco and

that whole stinky cheese saga. Why didn't I just tell her I didn't like cheese that tastes like puke? Or I could've said I was allergic to dairy. Why did I turn into such a sneaky jerk? Why did I pull the bag out of her hands like a seventh-grade bully?

Or if life had to offer such unpleasant moments, why weren't we equipped with an Undo key? Couldn't someone come up with an app that let you delete certain unwanted acts? I didn't want to Ctrl/Alt/Del meeting Coco—just my dumbass behavior with the damn cheese.

Dad was still talking. "When Antoni Gaudí finally passed his school exams, one of his professors said: 'Who knows if we have given this diploma to a nut or to a genius. Time will tell.'"

"Gaudí got the last laugh, huh?" I said.

Dad turned to me with a serious expression. "I want you to have a passion for something, Webb."

"No pressure, right?"

"None." He put an arm around my shoulder. "If you wanted to be a janitor, that would be fine with me, if that's what turned you on."

I loved Dad and his groovy lingo.

"I don't think I want to be a janitor," I informed him. "I don't think I'm tidy enough."

"Okay," Dad said. "You don't have to know what you want to be. That comes later. But I want you to *want* more than just having a job and muddling through life. I want you to find a passion you believe in strongly enough to risk humiliation and rejection."

If Dad only knew the humiliation and rejection I'd found in Paris.

We continued the discussion in the cab to dinner.

"If you think about it, Jimmy Webb and Antoni Gaudí have a lot in common," Dad was saying. "Both were hugely talented guys who could've taken the easy route, writing forgettable songs and designing adequate buildings that were easy to like. But they didn't do that."

"Uh-huh."

Dad was on a roll. He went on like this for the entire cab ride, right until we pulled up in front of a restaurant.

"They took risks. Webb. I can't tell you how important it is to take risks in life. To be bold. Because if you do that—"

I stopped listening. The air felt different. The night had changed. I felt it as soon as we stepped out of the cab and onto the sidewalk. I felt it before I could even see it. But as soon as my eyes focused, there it was: the oddly familiar swirl of colors in front of me, chest high.

The peasant blouse.

Coco.

Oh, God.

CHAPTER 58

Coco

O h, shit!"

"Coco!" Mom hissed, elbowing me in the ribs. Then she waved to Webb and an older guy. They were getting out of a cab together. "Andrew! Hello! I want you to meet my daughter, Coco."

The man shook my hand. "Very nice to meet you. And I'd like you both to meet Webb, my son."

He was wearing a navy blue jacket and jeans. "Hi," he said blankly.

"Hi," I echoed.

Jesus Christ. Was this really happening? No, it was a dream. It had to be a dream. Life wasn't like this. But wait, Webb was in color! Everything was in color. So this was real.

"Do you, Coco?" Mom was saying.

"What?" I mumbled.

Why was I wearing these dorky black pants? I hated them. And I didn't have on any makeup. Argh! I could kill Mom.

"Andrew asked if you were enjoying Barcelona," Mom said in her be-nice-to-the-distinguished-old-dude voice.

"Sure," I said. I looked again at Webb to see if it was really him.

How did he get here? How did Mom know his dad?

"We spent the afternoon at Casa Batlló," Mom was saying. "Just like you suggested."

"Webb loves that house," the man said. "Don't you, Webb?"

"Uh-huh," Webb answered. He wasn't even looking at me.

"Shall we see if our table's ready?" the man asked. He held the door open for Mom and me.

"Yes, let's," Mom said, smiling and moving toward the restaurant entrance.

"Yeah," I said, trying to remember how to put one foot in front of the other.

"What a pretty blouse you're wearing, Coco," the older guy said as I walked by. I spun around like a swivel head and looked at Webb. He was staring at his feet and grinning wildly.

CHAPTER 59

Andrew

I loved knowing that whatever else Coco's father was, he was a genetic lightweight.

Coco looked exactly like her mother. The same chestnut-colored hair. The identical thin nose. If I ever got to know this young woman, I would enjoy telling her that she needn't fear getting older. Her mother was proof positive of that.

The maître d' led us to a table and helped Daisy with her chair. I tried to send a message with my eyes to Webb that he could help Coco in the same manner, but it was pointless. He wasn't even looking at her. He was staring at the napkins on the table with a vacant expression on his face.

"I like this place already," Daisy said, admiring the stone walls. "Mmmmm, smell that garlic."

"I was nervous choosing a restaurant for us," I confessed.

Then I turned to Webb. "Daisy's a chef in Chicago. And I have it on good authority that she's the best in town."

Daisy smiled modestly. She looked gorgeous in a cream silk blouse. Silk blouses were clearly part of her uniform. I loved that she traveled light. My mind spun ahead to the trips we might take together. Rome. Edinburgh. Prague. Tokyo.

"I'm going to need some help translating," Daisy said, opening the menu. "I don't even recognize these words. Is this Spanish?"

"Catalan," I said. "Webb knows more than I do. He's been studying it on his own for a few years. Right, Webb?"

No response.

"And this really is a terrific restaurant," I said. "One of our favorites, I'd say, wouldn't you, Webb?"

Still no response. I felt like throttling him.

Try! Connect! Join the conversation. Pretend these are people you meet on the Internet. Put yourself out there, for God's sake!

I ordered a bottle of red wine for Daisy and me. "The seafood here is delicious," I said. "Do you like seafood, Coco? I bet you have a more sophisticated palate than most of your classmates."

No response from her, either.

This could be a very long evening.

CHAPTER 60

Daisy

Coco," I said, trying to sound nicer than I felt. "Andrew asked you a question. About your *palate*."

"Do what?" she said.

Why is she acting like such a dope? She was usually at her best when she had an audience. So why isn't she turning it on for Andrew and his completely adorable son?

"Your *palate*," I repeated. She knew what this meant. She just wasn't trying. Maybe I should've told her this was a date. For *me*.

"Oh," Coco said. "My palate is . . . pretty average, I'd say."

"I don't know if I agree with that," I said. "Remember the macaroni and cheese incident at school?"

"Oh, yeah," Coco said, her face brightening. "I got sent home from school once because the macaroni and cheese in the cafeteria made me cry. But it *is* vile stuff."

"I agree," I said, studying the menu.

"What's wrong with mac and cheese?" Webb asked.

I could see Andrew folding into his chair. "Is that the hideous orange stuff you make me buy?" he asked.

"I like it," Webb said. "Especially with scrambled eggs. Dad, you like it, too."

"I, um—" Andrew began. "I'll admit that in a pinch, I've been known to—"

"Eat a whole box," Webb said, smiling.

I smiled, too, but Andrew looked uncomfortable. I needed to change the subject—quickly. I leaned over to Coco.

"Did you know," I began, "that Webb is named after Jimmy Webb? He was a songwriter who—"

"Yeah, I know," Coco said. " 'Galveston.' 'MacArthur Park.' 'Wichita Lineman.' "

"I'm impressed!" Andrew said. "How do you like that, Webb? And you say kids your age don't know who Jimmy Webb is."

I turned to Coco. "How do you know all those old songs?" She just shrugged.

The wine steward arrived and poured a taste for Andrew.

"Nice," said Andrew, sipping the wine. He turned to me. "Okay, try this one. Webb's middle name is the last name of a famous architect."

"Wright?" I asked.

"Wrong," Andrew said.

"Let me think," I said. "Um . . ."

Oh, great. I'm blanking out. All the architects in the world and the only one I can think of is Frank Lloyd Wright.

"It's not Buckminster Fuller, is it?" I tried.

"Nope," Andrew said.

"Oh, wait." I laughed. "Sullivan? As in Louis Sullivan?"

"No," said Webb. "But good guess."

"Van der Rohe?" I said.

"Nope." Andrew was grinning. So was Webb. I was grateful for the generous pour from the steward.

"Come on, Coco," I said, taking a sip, "Help me out here."

"Is it . . . Gaudí?" she asked.

Andrew clapped his hands and knocked over the bottle of wine. The blood red liquid splashed all over my new silk blouse.

"Dammit!" he said, grabbing his napkin and aiming for my breasts. "I'm so sorry. Can I help you—"

"It's fine," I said, waving away the stain with a nonchalance that surprised even me. "Please, don't worry about it."

CHAPTER 61

Webb

As she stared at her mother, Coco's raised eyebrows reminded me that this was the woman who spent a ton of money on clothes.

I knew instantly what Coco was thinking because I was thinking it, too. *Something is up with our parents.*

"So how do you guys know each other?" I asked.

"Yeah, like what's *up* with you two?" Coco added quickly.

"Remember the favor I did for Solange?" Coco's mom said. "Fixing party food for that museum gala in Madrid? Andrew was the designer for the exhibit."

Dad turned to me. "Webb, you know the cookies and gooey butter cake served on opening night?"

"Yeah?" I said cautiously. Because I had no idea what he was talking about.

"Daisy made those," Dad said. "Er, I should say, Ms. Sprinkle."

"Daisy's fine," Coco's mom said. She was almost as pretty as her daughter.

The waiter arrived to take our order. I looked at the menu, but it had morphed into a Hieronymus Bosch painting filled with tiny, giddy figures tangled in a human knot.

CHAPTER 62

Coco

I could tell Webb was trying to connect the dots, just like I was. If my mom and his dad knew each other, did that mean they also knew about *us*?

It didn't seem possible. Mom was acting so nicey nice. She'd be in flames if she knew I'd lied to her about being sick to get out of going to Madrid.

Then again, she *did* seem to be prodding me lately to fess up to something.

I looked at her more closely. She was staring at Webb's dad. She was laughing and batting her eyelashes like a cartoon character.

That's when it hit me: Was this old guy my *father*? I nearly choked on my water.

"Honey, are you okay?" Mom asked.

"Yeah," I said. "Fine."

I'd always assumed my dad was French. But maybe he

was American. Why couldn't a master chef working in Paris nineteen years ago have been an American?

I took a breath. "So exactly how long have you two known each other?"

Webb's dad looked at Mom and smiled. My heart sank. And then it fluttered.

Wait a minute. If Webb knew his dad was also *my* dad, that would explain why he hadn't wanted to have tantric sex with me. I was his sister!

Oh. My. God! This was like a weird-ass European edition of *The Parent Trap*!

"We met on Tuesday night," Mom said.

Shit.

CHAPTER 63

Andrew

The food arrived and I'm sure it was delicious. But I had no appetite. Not for food, anyway.

I couldn't take my eyes off Daisy. Even in her wine-splattered blouse, she looked radiant. Webb seemed to like her, too.

"Do you know how to make crème brûlée?" he asked over dessert.

"Sure," she said. As Daisy began to explain the process to Webb in the most wonderful and encouraging way ("It's easy if you have the right tools"), I couldn't help reaching under the table and placing my hand on her knee. She looked surprised, but also—*was it too crazy to think?*—pleased.

"Crème brûlée is a great dessert to serve tableside," Daisy was saying. "As long as you don't set your guests on fire."

"Has that ever happened?" Webb asked, a strange delight in his eyes.

Please ignore my son's fascination with fire. He's really quite harmless.

"No," Daisy answered. "But you have to be careful with the torch. Isn't that right, Coco?"

"Mom's referring to the time I almost burned our house down. I was trying to make baked Alaska."

"You know how to make baked Alaska?" Webb asked. "With flames and everything?"

Please stop acting like a pyromaniac.

"Yeah," said Coco. "It's not hard to make."

"Seriously?" Webb said.

"Coco, why don't you e-mail Webb the recipe when we get home?" Daisy suggested.

She withdrew from her bag a pen and a small silver case containing business cards.

"Here you go," Daisy said, handing cards to both Webb and Coco. "Exchange e-mail addresses so you can keep in touch."

She replaced the case in her purse. Then she made a face at something she saw in her bag. She pulled out a piece of folded paper and handed it to me. I recognized it instantly, but reread it to torture myself.

Dear Ms. 6B,

Please forgive my clumsiness while boarding. I would be more than happy to pay for the cleaning or replacement of your blouse. Truth is, I would be even happier if you'd let me take you to dinner sometime when we return to our side of the pond. That is, if you do plan to return to the U.S. (For all I know, you could be Parisian. You have That Look.)

Were I traveling alone, I might be bolder and introduce myself to you. But for now, all I can do is invite you to e-mail me if you're interested in meeting an admirer who feels terrible about ruining your travel attire.

> Most sincerely,
> Mr. 13C
> My E-mail: lineman@com

P.S. You are truly first class.

CHAPTER 64

Daisy

That's the thing I was telling you about," I whispered to Andrew as he unfolded the note.

I was trying to be cryptic because I hadn't told Coco about my creepy secret admirer and didn't plan to. I didn't want her to be any more afraid of dating than she already was.

I watched Webb and Coco trade e-mail addresses. If I wasn't completely blind, there was something between them. A spark of interest, perhaps? Or maybe just a bit of healthy curiosity.

"So, yeah, e-mail me sometime, Mr. Nelson," Coco said coolly.

"I might just do that, Ms. Sprinkle," Webb said.

"Please do," Coco said, batting her eyelashes like a soap opera vixen. "I'll be home late Saturday night."

"Me, too," Webb said. "We're flying from Paris tomorrow."

They joked and laughed about flight schedules and the

merits of checking or not checking luggage. I couldn't help silently rejoicing. Coco was being *nice.* Her weeklong cranky attitude was apparently directed only at me—and not the whole world. This was huge. This was cause for celebration. She would do fine at college—and in life. My work was done!

And Andrew's son was adorable. Maybe Webb was bringing out the best in Coco.

"You guys should trade e-mail addresses, too," Coco said, looking from me to Andrew.

"Of course, how rude of me," I said, pulling out my card case and retrieving another business card. I handed it to Andrew. "Now you know where to find me online."

But Andrew continued to stare as if in disbelief at the handwritten note I'd given him. With an odd expression on his face, he folded the note and returned it to me.

"Dad, give her your e-mail address," Webb said.

"I . . . don't use e-mail very much," Andrew said, signaling for the waiter to bring the check.

Webb burst out laughing. "Yeah, right, Mr. Chained-to-His-BlackBerry."

Andrew cleared his voice. "I mean, I *used* to. But I'm really trying to connect more. With people. You know, face-to-face connections. Or sometimes the phone. Or—"

"What are you *talking* about?" Webb interrupted. "You don't even turn off your BlackBerry when you go to bed. Remember when we first got to Madrid? You were getting up in the middle of the night to check e-mail. So give her your e-mail address."

I felt my chest tighten. The room was starting to spin. I put my hands on the table to steady myself.

"*Da-ad*," Webb pressed. "*Give* her your e-mail address."

Andrew's face was locked in a pained expression. "I'm afraid I can't. If you'll excuse me, I'm going to find our waiter."

He left the table.

Of course he had somebody back home. Of course he did. Or maybe he had someone in Madrid. Maybe somebody in Barcelona, too. And Paris.

Why had I been such an idiot? Why was I so stupid?

Oh God, I'm having a heart attack.

Breathe. Breathe. Breathe.

"It's time to go, Coco," I said, standing up.

It's not a heart attack, I told myself. It's only anxiety. And anxiety is just unexpressed anger.

"Wait," Webb said, looking around the restaurant for his missing dad. "Can you wait till my dad—"

"No," I said. "We're leaving."

Who are you angry with? Nobody. I'm really not angry. I'd explained this to Nancy a million times.

Yes, you are angry. Who are you mad at? I'm not mad! I'm just tired. Tired of the whole damn thing.

"Where are you guys staying?" Webb asked. "Maybe we could take a cab back together. I think Dad's just paying the bill."

"Tell him we said thank you," I snapped. "Come on, Coco. Let's go."

CHAPTER 65

Webb

Dad looked terrible when he got back to the table.

"Yeow, did you get sick?" I asked.

"No," he replied. "Where are—"

"They left. Daisy said to tell you thank you."

I didn't tell him how she'd said it. I didn't have the heart to tell him how I'd screwed up his chances with this woman he obviously liked.

I was pretty sure what had happened. When Coco and I were pretending to trade e-mail addresses—as if I didn't have CocoChi@com tattooed on my brain—Coco must've given her mom the "We're *out* of here" look.

I'd known since middle school how girls had all these secret codes and eye signals. Coco probably gave her mom the "If you think I would ever go *out* with this guy, you're insane" signal.

Whatever the message was, they were gone. And Dad was sick about it.

"Sorry," I said.

"It's not your fault."

It is so my fault, I wanted to say. I wished I could tell him the whole story, but I couldn't. It would take too long, and he'd get mad. And it didn't really matter now because I'd screwed up this thing he was trying to get going with Daisy, who seemed pretty damn great, like her daughter. Coco looked even prettier than she had in Paris. She was funnier, too. And once we got past the initial shock of seeing each other, I thought it was going pretty well.

Obviously I was wrong.

So, let's see, not only did I bungle any chance I had with Coco, I'd also spoiled Dad's chances with Coco's mom.

What an idiot.

CHAPTER 66

Coco

"M o-om," I repeated for the tenth time in the cab back to the hotel. "What'd I do? Just *tell* me what I did wrong. I'd actually like to know."

"*Actually*, everything isn't *about* you," she said, staring out her side of the cab. "I know you might find that hard to believe, but it's true. The world doesn't revolve around you."

Right. She was obviously mad at me for flirting with Webb. It was 100 percent obvious. Part of me wanted to tell her the whole stupid story so she'd know that I *knew* him already, and we were just goofing. But then I'd have to deal with her getting mad about *how* I knew him.

We rode the rest of the way to the hotel in silence.

"Did Webb say they were flying to Chicago on a five o'clock flight from Paris?" Mom asked as we walked in the lobby.

"Yeah, I think so. Why?"

"I need to change something," Mom announced. She

marched straight to the concierge desk and began making arrangements to get us on a different flight.

"Mother," I said as calmly as I could. "Don't you think you're overreacting just a *little* bit?"

"No," she replied. She was staring straight ahead. "We're done here."

"Fine," I said. "Be that way. Throw a complete hissy fit just because the poor dude doesn't have e-mail. I hate to tell you this, but it's not like you're a real computer whiz yourself. You still don't know how to text very fast. And I've seen you write e-mail in all caps, which is considered completely *rude*."

Mom turned to face me. The wine stain on her blouse looked like a gunshot wound.

"*Rude?*" she asked. "You have the gall to lecture *me* on being rude?"

"Yeah," I started to say. "Because—"

"Go up to the room," she said. "I can't deal with you right now."

CHAPTER 67

Andrew

*I*f only I'd told her about the note in the bar after the exhibit opening. Or how about if I just hadn't written the goddamn note in the first place? How about that? Or how about if I weren't such a first-class *ass*?

These were the thoughts that crashed like waves in my head later that night at the hotel.

"Are we going back to Madrid?" Webb asked. He was in bed, but not sleeping.

"No," I said. "We're just an hour or so away from Paris now. I've booked us to fly into Paris early tomorrow morning. And then we'll catch our flight home from there."

"Great," said Webb. "We'll see Coco and Daisy again. They're on the same flight to Chicago."

"They are?"

"Yeah. Didn't you hear Coco and me talking?"

I didn't hear anything after Daisy handed me the note.

I knew I couldn't face her again. Not until I could explain why I had refused to give her my e-mail address, which meant coming clean about the note, which meant utter humiliation.

If I really cared about her as much as I thought I did, I should have the courage to risk looking like a fool. But I couldn't. The very thing I'd been telling Webb he needed to learn, I couldn't do myself.

I used my BlackBerry to change our flight itinerary.

"Get some sleep," I told Webb as I confirmed seats on the 12:15 P.M. flight out of Paris. "We've got a long day in front of us."

CHAPTER 68

Daisy

Back in the room, Coco was acting pissy and I didn't care. I should've left her with my parents and taken a vacation by myself.

Now, after a week of putting up with her roller-coaster moods, I was stuck with the prospect of returning home to the inevitable questions about why I'd quit Bon Soir and where I'd be working next.

There were probably a half-dozen job offers waiting for me. Old restaurants. New restaurants. I had a loyal following. Restaurant owners knew I could bring in good business.

Or I could go the route of becoming a private chef for some moneybag couple on the Gold Coast who liked to entertain. Or I could send lunch over to Harpo Studios and go after a little green room business. Catering for celebrities was practically a cottage industry in Chicago.

"The world is your oysters Rockefeller," Solange had told me at the exhibit. "Decide what you want and go get it."

"What Does Daisy Sprinkle Want?" That stupid headline had ruined my vacation.

What *did* I want? I wanted to stop falling for jerks like Andrew. I wanted to stop getting my hopes up like a pathetic teenage girl worrying about prom.

Nancy thought I needed to spend more time in therapy. I thought I needed a small vacation. We were both wrong.

I needed to work. I was a person who was happiest when working. Because when I didn't work, I let my guard down. And look what happened: Andrew.

I was still fizzing with rage and indignation, but now I felt a dull headache start to take shape in the space behind my eyes. I thought about calling Solange and telling her the whole story. But then she'd feel obligated to feel sorry for me, and I didn't feel like being pitied at the moment.

It was humiliating to think I'd gotten my hopes up over Andrew. It must've been jet lag. I'd lost my game for a few days. There was something in the water in Europe that made me drop my guard. It'd happened during culinary school and now again with Andrew. I knew I'd get my groove back. But still. Damn him and his "Sorry, I can't give you my e-mail" bullshit. I felt sorry for whoever he was seeing. No, I didn't. I felt jealous. No, I didn't. I pitied her. Poor thing. Poor fool. Poor stupid woman who didn't know her man was hitting on another woman.

I thought back to the look on his face when he was reading

the note from my secret admirer. He looked ashen. Almost ghostlike.

Wait a minute. Did Andrew think *I* had somehow encouraged that creepy guy who wrote the note? Did he think I was a flirt? A slut?

The nerve of men. I took two Excedrins and crawled into bed.

At least I wouldn't have to see him again. The concierge had changed our flight reservations out of Paris from five o'clock to twelve fifteen.

Day 7: Saturday

AmericanAirlines
BOARDING PASS
ANDREW R. NELSON
FROM:
Paris - CDG
TO:
Chicago - ORD
FLIGHT
41
SEAT
23B
DEPARTS
12:15PM
ARRIVES
2:24PM
DATE CLASS
APRIL23

AmericanAirlines
BOARDING PASS
DAISY M. SPRINKLE
FROM:
Paris - CDG
TO:
Chicago - ORD
FLIGHT
41
SEAT
10B
DEPARTS
12:15PM
ARRIVES
2:24PM
DATE CLASS
APRIL23 P

Solange,

You're a dream to let us stay here.
Lots to talk about when you come to Chicago.
xxoo Daisy and Coco

AmericanAirlines
BOARDING PASS
WEBB G. NELSON
FROM:
Paris - CDG
TO:
Chicago - ORD
FLIGHT
41
SEAT
23A
DEPARTS
12:15PM
ARRIVES
2:24PM
DATE CLASS
APRIL23

AmericanAirlines
BOARDING PASS
COCO L. SPRINKLE
FROM:
Paris - CDG
TO:
Chicago - ORD
FLIGHT
41
SEAT
10A
DEPARTS
12:15PM
ARRIVES
2:24PM
DATE CLASS
APRIL23 P

CHAPTER 69

Webb

When I woke up, Dad was on the phone, ordering room service coffee.

"Don't you want to see your friend?" I asked. "She'll probably be downstairs having breakfast."

"I'll pass," he said in a gloomy voice. "But you should go get something to eat. We have to leave for the airport soon."

"You're not going to stay in the room, are you?" I asked. But Dad didn't answer.

I dressed and went downstairs. As soon as I walked in the hotel dining room, I saw Coco's mom sitting at a table by the window. She was alone, drinking coffee and reading a newspaper. I took a deep breath and walked over to her table.

"Hey," I said quietly.

"Webb," she answered, putting the paper on the table and smiling. Then she frowned. "Is your dad here?"

"No, he's upstairs."

"Oh." She seemed to relax.

I had to think fast. "Dad wanted me to tell you you're welcome," I lied.

"What?"

"Remember when you told me to thank him last night? For dinner? I did, and he said, 'She's very welcome.' "

"Oh," she said again. This time she lowered her eyes.

It was no use. I'd ruined whatever chance they had. Coco had tipped her off that I was an idiot. So, by extension, whoever raised me was also an idiot.

"Have you eaten yet?" she asked. "There's a nice selection of pastries over there."

I followed the direction of her hand. "Thanks. That sounds good."

I walked over to the buffet where I removed two croissants from a platter and put them on a napkin. I glanced back at Daisy. She was reading the newspaper.

I got the hint and left.

CHAPTER 70

Coco

M om was in such a lousy mood that morning that I took my croissant to the hotel business center, where I finally had a chance to do what I'd wanted to do since I saw Webb at the restaurant.

Fr: CocoChi@com
To: Webbn@com
Subject: Okay, here goes...

Dear Webb,

I am still trying to wrap my frazzled brain around what happened—not just in Paris, but here in Barcelona. And I wish I could laugh about it. But the truth is, I feel like such a bitch. You came all the way from Madrid on a train to see me, and what did I do but YELL at you? If I tell you the reason, will you promise not to laugh? (I'm going to have to imagine you promising.) Okay, so here's what happened. My mother (who I can't believe you've now MET) somehow persuaded me to pack all my worst, most stretched-out, most pathetic underwear. Stuff I never wear. Stuff I never should've bought. Take, for example, that pink foam-padded bra that practically leaped out of my bag when you opened it. I think I wore that bra once—as a joke. Maybe twice. Or three times, at the very most. I only bought it because some girls in my class thought it would be funny to

The door to the business center opened.

"Hey, Coco," Webb said. "Wanna croissant?"

"Webb!" I screamed.

And with one click, I deleted the e-mail.

CHAPTER 71

Andrew

I found myself checking out of the hotel right behind Daisy. I considered asking if she wanted to share a cab to the airport. But why? So I could ruin yet another blouse? I had screwed this thing up so thoroughly I didn't have the courage now to be even polite.

And yet I couldn't resist staring at her as Webb and I waited for a cab outside the hotel. She was wearing the same black jacket she'd worn on the flight from Chicago—this time, over a T shirt. Probably Coco's.

I tried to smile as the two of them climbed in a cab. *I will never see her again,* I thought. *Never. Ever. Ever.*

Naturally, an hour and a half later, I saw her on the plane. I barely had the nerve to look up as Webb and I walked past her and Coco on our humiliating way back to coach.

As the plane took off, I closed my eyes. The show had been

a success. That was the reason I'd come to Spain. That and spending time with Webb during his spring break.

I opened my eyes and looked at Webb. He was sitting across the aisle from me and staring straight ahead. *Zoning out,* as he called it.

I thought back to the night in the hotel bar when Daisy and I had talked about our kids. It was such a rare and welcome exchange of parental fears. But why did I tell her the whole sorry saga about my sister? I barely knew Daisy. And yet I'd felt an immediate connection with her. She was strong and confident, but also warm and caring. I wondered if she'd minded when I touched her knee under the table at dinner. She didn't seem to, judging from the look on her face.

But that face was long gone now, never to resurface again in my company. This was a woman who had banished steak sauce—a condiment!—and waged a jihad against televisions in bars. She was a person who didn't suffer fools, and I admired her for that.

I just wished I hadn't been such a fool.

CHAPTER 72

Daisy

As awkward as the whole stupid situation had become, there simply wasn't time to worry about it on the flight from Barcelona to Paris. When we landed, we had to get from the airport to Solange's apartment so we could pick up Coco's bag and the rest of my stuff, and then back to the airport—all in two hours.

"Depechez-vous, s'il vous plaît," I said several times to the cab driver.

"I cannot understand you," he said in a thick, unidentifiable accent.

"I'm trying to ask you to *hurry*," I said. "Please."

"I am attempting it, of course," he barked. "But Cinco por Cinco. Quelle horreur."

Only then did I notice the protesters marching down the

center of the street, holding their hand-shaped signs and tying up traffic. I remembered the newspaper article Andrew had read to me about the Amish extremists, subsisting on a diet of water and uncooked oats.

Maybe they have a point, I thought. I'd been eating buttery croissants all week and was feeling the effects on my waistline.

When we finally arrived at Solange's apartment, I threw fifty euros at the driver and asked him to wait ten minutes. Coco and I raced up to the apartment. While she gathered her gear, I quickly tidied the place: wiping down the kitchen counter, scouring the sink, throwing a set of clean sheets on my bed. I scribbled a note and left it on Solange's desk.

Solange,

You're a dream to let us stay here.
Lots to talk about when you come to Chicago.
                              xxoo Daisy and Coco

I was surprised to find the taxi still waiting outside. Of course the driver couldn't be bothered to load our luggage for us. But at least he waited while Coco and I crammed our bags in the dirty trunk and then settled ourselves in the backseat of the cab.

By the time Coco and I were finally sitting on the plane to Chicago, I was too exhausted to be bothered by the sight of Andrew and Webb boarding. I simply smiled at Webb and ignored his asshole of a father.

Chuck That.

The plane was full and noisy. Flight attendants prodded lagging passengers to hurry along.

"The plane cannot depart until everyone is seated," a flight attendant said. She was a tired-looking woman, probably my age, who looked inordinately sick of life. Or maybe she was just sick of her job. Sick of people. Sick of travel. Even the scarf around her neck drooped a bit.

As soon as everyone was seated, the pilot made an announcement from the cockpit.

"Ladies and gentlemen, this is your captain speaking," he reported. "Our departure time has been pushed back. We have been ordered to comply with this nonmechanical delay."

I couldn't help groaning.

"Can I get you something while we're waiting?" the tired-looking flight attendant asked dully. "Coffee, juice, water—"

"I'll take a couple of those little bottles of cabernet, please," I said. Then, trying to be considerate I added, "In fact, bring me three and I won't ask for another thing until we land."

She handed me a depressing fistful of miniature bottles without making eye contact. I turned to see what Coco wanted to drink, but her eyes were closed. She'd been quiet all morning. Nothing new there. I chalked it up to her general moodiness. Then it hit me: *This was her prom night.*

Poor kid. Why couldn't I cut her some slack? She and her friends had been e-mailing all week about the drama surrounding prom. (Did Coco really think I didn't know where she was going on those alleged trips to the patisserie?)

And yet Coco refused to admit that any of this bothered her. Maybe it didn't. I hoped it didn't.

Then again, wouldn't it have been fun for her to get dressed up and go on a date—a *real* date—with a nice kid like Webb? I loved the sweet and awkward way he'd approached my table at breakfast. I applauded his respect for my privacy, even though I tried to make it clear with my body language that he wouldn't be bothering me if he wanted to eat his croissants at my table. ("Look," I tried to say with my eyes. "I'm just reading the paper. I won't bite!") He was a sweet boy. It wasn't his fault that his dad was an ass.

The pilot was making another announcement. "We have been told to expect an indefinite delay. Please remain seated. Passengers are not allowed to move from their ticketed seats. However, cellular phones may be used while we are detained."

I remembered Solange's cell phone. I reached under the seat in front of me and pulled the phone from my bag. When I turned it on, a closed envelope icon indicated I had a message. I clicked on the icon.

Fr: Solange@com
To: DaisyS@com
Subject: Fine

Daisy: I am fine. Will call soon. Andrew = perfect for you.

I fumbled around with the phone until I found the reply button.

Fr: DaisyS@com
To: Solange@com
Subject: Re: Fine

> *No, he's not perfect for me. But it's OK. Fine, in
> fact.*
> *Everything's just fine.*

I stared at the last line. *Just fine.*

My tired brain twisted it into a headline: "Daisy Sprinkle's Just Fine. But Thanks for Asking."

What a load of shit, as Coco would say. And she would be right.

I could feel my eyes burning. I wished the damn plane would take off already so I could get away from this stupid continent.

I started to put the phone back in my purse, but then saw, once again, that ridiculous note from Mr. 13C.

I reread it. And then with hot tears in my eyes, I responded to Lineman@com.

It was, perhaps, the truest thing I'd ever written.

CHAPTER 73

Webb

*O*h, God.

Eight cops carrying automatic weapons were boarding the plane.

I turned to Dad. "What the hell?"

"I don't know," he said.

For several minutes we had no clue what was going on, other than the fact that we were in the middle of something serious. Finally, there was an announcement.

"This is your captain speaking. We have received an order that this aircraft will be detained while security measures are enforced."

I looked at Dad. "It's okay," he said. "I'm sure it's nothing." He was a terrible liar.

One of the cops began giving directions in French, English, and then Spanish.

"All cell phones and mobile communications devices must now be turned off while we conduct our investigation," the cop said, walking to the back of the plane. "Please have no worries about the dogs. They know what they are doing."

Two hyperactive search dogs were released at the front of the plane. They made their way toward the back, sniffing every row.

"What are they looking for?" I whispered to Dad.

"Drugs, I guess," he said.

But this looked more serious than a simple drug bust. "Should we get off?" I asked, panicking. "Let's just fly home tomorrow."

"They won't let us off now," Dad said. "Relax. It's probably nothing serious."

The dogs were at our row, sniffing like crazed anteaters.

"All cell phones, BlackBerrys, iPhones, and pagers must be turned off," the cop said.

I looked at Dad and then at his BlackBerry.

He nodded. "It's off."

A second team of dogs had started working the other side of the plane.

"Whatever they're looking for, I don't think they're finding it," I said.

The plane was buzzing with excitement. Even the flight attendants looked rattled. I heard a note of anxiety in the pilot's voice when he made the next announcement.

"This is your captain speaking. The police have informed me that there have been numerous terrorist incidents across Europe today."

Screams and gasps of disbelief made the next part hard to hear.

"Shhhh," a flight attendant said, holding a finger to her mouth. "Be calm. Listen!"

"Residue from an explosive material has been detected in a piece of luggage that was checked for this flight," the captain continued. "The bag was not marked, so the police will need to question passengers on this flight."

CHAPTER 74

Coco

*O*h, *shit.*

The cops were everywhere.

"Attention," the main cop said in a French accent. He was trying to be a hard-ass, but he was using a dinky microphone to amplify his voice. My old karaoke machine had better sound than his contraption.

"Should I be scared?" I asked Mom.

"No," she said. "They'll find whatever it is they're looking for, and that will be that."

The hard-ass cop was fumbling with his Mister Microphone. "We can protect the passengers on this aircraft only if we have complete cooperation. Please, be calm so we can investigate this matter without injury."

A younger cop came on board. He was wearing gloves and carrying a gray plastic bin with a piece of luggage in it.

A black L.L.Bean duffel bag.

Oh, shit. Oh, shit. Oh, shit.

Officer Hard-Ass pointed at the bag. "Who does this bag belong to?" he demanded. "Come forward if this is your bag."

No one moved, including me. I felt paralyzed in my seat.

"Whose bag is this?" Hard-Ass continued in a louder voice. He motioned for the younger cop to unzip the bag. Then, with gloves on, Officer Hard-Ass reached inside. The first thing he pulled out? My freakin' pink foam-padded bra.

"This . . . *item* . . . belongs to a woman, perhaps?" Hard-Ass asked, waving my stupid bra over his head for all the world to see. "Or possibly a man."

Mom looked at me in disbelief. "Coco, is that *your*—"

And in that instant, I completely fell apart. "Mom," I cried. "*Do* something. Please. I'll *never* get into the undergraduate honors program now."

I was sobbing. My tears made everything look shiny and bubble shaped. Mom stood up and raised her hand.

"Excuse me," she said. "Hello! That bra you're holding belongs to my daughter. That's her bag. I thought it was properly identified." Mom turned to me. "Didn't you have your name on your bag?"

"It's in the side pocket," I said.

"Oh, right," Mom said. She cleared her throat and spoke directly to Officer Hard-Ass. "In any case, I can assure you that—"

Hard-Ass snapped his fingers at his underlings and then pointed at Mom and me.

"Detain them," he ordered. "They are perhaps terrorists."

"*Terrorists?*" Mom said.

"Actually," I said. But then I stopped because Mom was glaring at me. "Er, not *actually,* but just . . . What I'm trying to say is, there's been a huge mistake."

"No mistake," Officer Hard-Ass said. "We have found bomb residue inside your bag. Come with us now peacefully, or we will detain you with force."

"Wait!"

It was Webb. He was running from the back of the plane.

"*Arrêtez!*" yelled Officer Hard-Ass. "*Arrêtez!*"

"Webb, he's telling you to *stop,*" I called.

But Webb kept running. Hard-Ass grabbed his gun.

"Webb, stop!" I yelled.

"But I can explain everything," he said. "Please!"

"What is it you want to explain?" Officer Hard-Ass demanded.

Webb took a deep breath and then started talking really fast. "I put some sparklers in Coco's bag. Look in the very bottom."

Officer Hard-Ass grabbed my bag from the young cop and began pawing through it. Sure enough, seconds later he pulled out five sparklers.

"I bought them on the street in Madrid," Webb said. "I thought it'd be fun to light one the first time we kissed in Paris."

"Kissed?" Mom said. "*Paris?*" She turned to Officer Hard-Ass. "He means Barcelona. We had dinner together last night in Barcelona and—"

Webb was still talking. "And if we did something else, well, I thought it'd be cool to light a sparkler then, too."

"Something *else*?" I asked, sniffling. "Like what?"

"I don't know," Webb said quietly. "We never got around to something else because you thought I was an idiot."

"*I* was the idiot," I whispered. "I was a complete freakazoid. You were great."

"Really?" Webb asked. "You thought I was great? Because I thought *you* were great."

"Seriously?" I said.

Officer Hard-Ass cleared his throat. "It appears someone thought someone was *great* enough to need these," he announced, pulling a box of condoms from the bottom of my bag.

"Coco!" Mom said.

"Oh, I put those in there, too," Webb said. "Just in case."

He smiled at me.

My hero.

Officer Hard-Ass made a sour expression. He was still rifling through my bag. "And the *fromage*?"

"Cheese?" I asked.

"Yes," Hard-Ass said. "There is the smell of fermenting cheese in this bag."

I looked at Webb.

"I have no idea what that's about," he said, shrugging.

One of the junior cops approached Officer Hard-Ass and whispered something in his ear. Hard-Ass spun around and yelled in French to another cop, who pulled a photograph from his pocket. He handed the picture to Hard-Ass, who held it next to Webb's face.

"*Sacrebleu,* it's him!" Officer Hard-Ass shouted. "The leader of Cinco por Cinco. Arrest him!"

And with that, they slapped a pair of handcuffs on Webb and pulled him off the plane.

CHAPTER 75

Andrew

O h hell, I thought as I followed Webb to the front of the plane. I wished he'd stop talking long enough for me to call my attorney.

But now we were being led to a private room inside the airport police station.

"There's been a mistake," I told the French-accented senior officer.

"Erreur," Daisy said, her voice cracking. She and Coco had been pulled off the plane along with Webb.

"Just tell us what's going on," Webb said, sounding calmer than either Daisy or me. "I have a right to know what I'm being accused of."

"There have been multiple terrorist threats and one serious explosion today," the officer said. "An Amish extremist group called Cinco por Cinco has claimed responsibility."

"Cinco por Cinco," Daisy said, looking at me. "Isn't that the group that was protesting outside the museum? The people who believe the Internet is Satan's toy?"

"You're right," I said. I turned to the lead officer and explained what we'd seen after the opening gala.

He listened to everything and then responded coldly. "An explosion destroyed the Crystal Palace two hours ago."

Daisy screamed. "Solange! We have to call her."

"There will be time for phone calls later," the officer said. "For now, we are here to discuss the role of this young man in the terrorist attack." He was staring at Webb. "My colleagues have been investigating you since Tuesday, when you tried to recruit four young men to join Cinco por Cinco in Madrid."

"Recruit people?" Webb said. "What are you talking about?"

"On Paseo del Prado," the officer said. "At two thirty on Tuesday morning."

"What evidence do you have?" Webb asked.

"Webb," I said. "Don't talk. Let me call—"

But the officer was waving pictures in front of Webb's face. "You want evidence? I give you evidence."

As Webb looked at the pictures, a glimmer of recognition passed over his face. "Oh, *that*. I was just buying sparklers from those guys. They were trying to rip me off. I wanted five sparklers for five euros. Cinco por cinco."

"I don't want to continue this conversation until we have a lawyer in the room," I announced, raising my voice for the first time.

"It's okay," Webb said. "I'm fine with this."

The officer continued. "When we finally identified you, we

began asking questions of those who know you in *San Luis,* Missouri."

I prayed Webb wouldn't laugh at the French pronunciation of our city. He didn't. To my surprise, he was listening intently and looking the officer directly in the eye.

"We spoke with several of your teachers," the officer said. "We learned that you do not drive."

"I like public transportation," Webb shot back. "And our driver's ed teacher is a sex maniac. Coco's driving teacher was a perv, too, for what it's worth."

The officer continued. "And according to Mademoiselle Fogerty, you are a fan of Henry David Thoreau, an American anarchist and a hero of the Cinco por Cinco movement because of his renunciation of technology and modern civilization."

"You talked to Miss Fogerty?" Webb asked.

Now it was Coco's turn. "For heaven's sake, he can *admire* Thoreau's writing without being a terrorist."

"Thanks, Coco," Webb said.

"You're welcome," she replied, smiling. Then she spoke directly to the officer. "If you knew Webb at all, you'd know that he wasn't antitechnology. He uses the Internet all the time."

The officer condescended to smile. "It is the nature of extremists that in the name of their cause they often embrace the thing they hate."

"Tell me about this explosion you think I caused," Webb demanded.

Oh, hell. He was practically admitting he'd done it. My mind reeled back to the scene at the police station after Laura admitted her role in the bank robbery. It was exactly the same: the sick feeling of dread combined with the realization that the person you loved the most could also be the person you knew least.

"Webb," I pleaded. "Please stop talking."

"No, Dad, really," Webb said, holding a hand up to me and motioning for the officer to continue. "Tell me what I did and how I did it. I'm curious."

"Our bomb investigation team has concluded that the low-tech explosive device that destroyed the Crystal Palace was planted on the night of the opening," the investigator stated.

Webb exhaled a huge sigh of relief. "Well, I'm sorry to hear that. But you'll be sorrier to know that I wasn't even there that night."

"Goddammit, Webb," I said under my breath. "This is serious. Stop screwing around."

"Dad, I'm not kidding. I wasn't there. I was in Paris."

"With me," Coco said. "And I can prove it!"

She pulled a digital camera from her bag and turned it around so we could see the pictures stored on it.

"See?" she said. "Here we are at an Internet café. The time and date are right there on the picture. And here we are with Glen Campbell."

"Glen Campbell?" Daisy said.

"Well, just his picture on YouTube," Coco explained. "And here are a couple more pictures of us." She handed the camera to the officer. "Oh, and just so you know, Webb and I exchanged bags. But we're still entitled to five hundred dollars from the airline. We *earned* it."

"Coco, please," Daisy said, squirming. "That has nothing to do with this."

The officer wasn't listening. He was too busy scowling as he clicked through Coco's digital images. Then he turned to me.

"But you say your son was with you on Tuesday night in Madrid."

"I thought he was," I admitted with equal parts joy and embarrassment. "He e-mailed me throughout the night, telling me how much he was enjoying the show."

"Sorry, Dad," Webb said. And then he explained how he'd programmed his e-mail account to send me messages so I wouldn't know he was gone.

By the time the inquisition ended, I didn't know who was more confused: me or our French interrogator. He finally released us after more than four hours of questioning—and after the real leader of Cinco por Cinco was apprehended in Madrid.

"We have to call Solange," Daisy said. We were walking, all four of us, with our bags through the terminal. I turned on my BlackBerry. I had two new messages.

Fr: Solange@com
To: Lineman@com
Subject: OK

Just in case you get this message before we talk, I am fine. I was having coffee on the Plaza Mayor with Maria Luciana when the explosion occurred. And to think I volunteered to curate a quilt show for those idiots! The

Crystal Palace is gone. The exhibit destroyed. But no deaths
or serious injuries, so that is good. I am trying to get in touch
with the police. The electrical contractor tells me the caterer
(remember? he said his father died?) was a member of Cinco
por Cinco—and hired "waiters," also members of Cinco
por Cinco, to dump many bags of oats down the toilets. The
septic system backed up resulting in a sewer gas explosion—
and a stinky mess. I suppose I need to start running
background checks on the people I hire, yes? Anyway, I am
on my way to Paris now. We will talk later. If you see Daisy,
tell her I am fine. I cannot get through to her on the cell.

I remembered the earlier problems with the toilets. I
thought someone had poured wet cement down them. Could
it have been oats? So this is what they meant by low-tech
terrorism.

I sent Solange a quick message ("Thank God you're okay.
We'll talk soon."). Then I opened my second message. I read
it, barely breathing.

Fr: DaisyS@com
To: Lineman@com
Subject: Why You're an Ass (continued)

*I didn't have time before—and perhaps I wasn't in
the proper frame of mind—to fully respond to the note
you left in my bag. But I have a few moments now,
and there's something I'd like to tell you. It's about
a boyfriend I had in college. We agreed before we*

left school for the summer that we'd keep in touch by writing letters. I lived in Chicago. He lived in Rhode Island. He wrote me one letter in early June. I wrote him probably 20 letters. And I kept writing, waiting for him to write back. Or call. We'd agreed back at school that we'd call each other and hang up after one ring—because neither of us had money for long-distance phone calls back then, and the phone company doesn't charge for calls that don't get answered. But he never called me. Never. Not even a one-ringer. How do I know this? Because I sat next to the damn phone all summer long. And when I went back to college in the fall, I found out he'd moved in with an old girlfriend in the middle of June to "save money." Which meant I'd been calling and hanging up on somebody else's phone all summer long. And even worse than that, I'd gotten my hopes up that someone out there was thinking about me; someone who needed me more than he wanted me. (I'm referring to a line from a Jimmy Webb song. Never mind. You wouldn't understand.) My point is, I was crazy about that guy. Emphasis on crazy. And I resolved that I would never again put myself in that situation—which resulted in my dating men I didn't especially want or need or even *like* for decades. But recently I met a guy who had a lot going for him: kind, handsome, good job, decent conversationalist. And he seemed to like me. (Always an admirable quality in a man.) And I'll be damned

*if I didn't get butterflies in my stomach every time he
called. He was funny. He was obviously a good father.
And a wonderful brother. And (AND!) I found out
last night that he has somebody back home. My point?
I fell into the same goddamn trap that I fell in when
I was 20 years old. And okay, maybe part of it's my
fault. Maybe I let my guard down. Maybe it was jet
lag. The fact that you were able to stick a note in my
bag without me noticing it suggests I haven't been
as careful lately as I should've been. So I take some
responsibility for that. But if it weren't for guys like
him and you and Chuck who hit on women when you
already HAVE someone at home—or someone you're
TRAVELING WITH, I wouldn't FALL into this trap.
Do you get it? Am I making myself clear? Some idiotic
reporter wrote a story with the headline "What Does
Daisy Sprinkle Want?" Can I tell you what I want?
I want to stop wanting things I can't have. I want to
stop falling for jerks I don't need. And I want to stop
feeling like an f/ing gooey butter cake somebody left
out in the rain, which is another Jimmy Webb reference
(also W. H. Auden) that you wouldn't understand,
you stupid, selfish, philandering coach-class jackass.*

CHAPTER 76

Daisy

Oh, please.

"How did you get my—" I started to say when Andrew handed me his BlackBerry. But then it hit me. "*You* put that note in my bag?"

He hung his head, but smiled in the affirmative. "Sorry?"

My brain absorbed the news while my body burned with the white heat of profound embarrassment. Andrew and I were walking behind Coco and Webb, who seemed to have a lot to say to each other now that they had explained everything to us.

"And the person you were traveling with was . . . Webb?" I asked.

"Yes," he said. "And Solange is fine. She thinks the caterer was behind the explosion."

"The guy who backed out at the last minute?"

"Right. He was the reason she asked you to help, remember? Kismet?"

"Kismet," I repeated softly.

I felt a solid lump of shame in my stomach. As I saw it, I had two options: one was to kill myself; the other was to change the subject.

"So how do we feel about the fact that our kids are escape artists?" I asked breezily.

"I don't know," Andrew answered. "Maybe I should be mad at Webb for what he did. But the truth is, I've never been prouder of him. Think how much effort he put into meeting Coco in Paris. It's impressive. And I thought your daughter wasn't a risk taker."

"I didn't think she was," I said, my mind still in a swirl. "I thought Webb had inertia."

"What do I know?" Andrew said. "I'm just his dad."

I smiled. "But what about the lies they told us? Doesn't that bother you?"

"A little," he said. "But in light of everything else, it seems a small price to pay. Speaking of prices, what was Coco saying about five hundred dollars from the airline?"

"Oh. Speaking of lies."

I told Andrew about the lie I'd told Coco. It was part of my new resolution, established in that moment, to be more honest with myself and everyone around me.

"It seemed worth five hundred dollars to buy her a better attitude," I confessed. "I was afraid her pissy mood was going to ruin my vacation."

"Why was she in a . . . pissy mood?"

"The age. It's not easy to be eighteen. Plus, her prom is this weekend. Tonight, in fact."

"Should I tell Webb?" he asked. "He could buy her some flowers. We're not going to get a flight out of here until tomorrow morning at the earliest. They could have a nice date tonight."

I looked at Coco walking with Webb. Her head was thrown back in laughter at something he was saying. "I think they're managing just fine without us," I said. "Besides, nobody dates anymore, remember? But speaking of dates."

"Do *you* want to go to prom tonight?" Andrew asked.

"No," I said, forcing a smile. "I don't date—not men I like, anyway."

"Why not?"

"Because I'm no good at it."

"I think you should let me be the judge of that," he said. "I had the best date of my life a few nights ago with you."

"*Really?*"

"Daisy, you're the most lovable person I've ever met."

"No, I'm not. I'm a hothead. I'm judgmental. I have a short fuse. Honestly, I don't even like being around myself most of the time."

"You're too hard on yourself."

"Don't you mean I'm too hard on other people?"

"Well, as only a 'pretty decent conversationalist,' I'm not sure I'm qualified to continue this conversation."

"Oh, God," I said, hiding my face behind one hand.

We walked in silence for a few steps before Andrew addressed the heart of my message.

"I knew that college boyfriend was no good," he said. "I just knew it."

I laughed nervously.

"I'm serious," he said. "Who could call you and let it ring once? And what if you'd answered? Would he have hung up on you?"

"Keep in mind, it was my idea," I replied. "And that he never called."

"That's beside the point," he said. "Any man who would agree to a plan like that is no good." He paused before continuing in a softer voice. "Why didn't you tell me the real story about what happened that summer?"

"I just remembered it last night. It all came back to me at the restaurant when you . . . well, you know." I tried to smile. "I told you I have relationship Alzheimer's."

"Yes, you did," he said. "And did I tell you that I'm not a one-ring-and-hang-up kind of guy?"

"No, I don't believe you did."

"Well, it's true. And there's something else." He stopped walking and turned to face me. "Remember when I called you at Solange's? How many times was it—three? Four?"

"Five," I said.

"Right. And do you know that with every phone call, when it was time to hang up, I could barely make myself do it? I stayed on the line long after you'd hung up."

"Really?"

"Every single time."

"You were still on the line, like the Wichita Lineman?"

He looked startled. "Is *that* what that song means?" He took a breath. "If it does, I'm him. The only difference is that I want you as much as I need you."

I elbowed him in the ribs. "You sure talk a smooth game, Mr. Lineman. I bet you say that to all the girls."

He shook his head. "I've never said that before to anybody."

An hour later, the four of us were climbing out of a taxi in Montmartre, where we found a shaky Solange unpacking her suitcase.

"Spend the night with me?" she asked, hugging us one by one. "I know this place is small, but—"

"No, it's perfect!" insisted Coco. "It'll be like a slumber party."

"Exactly," said Solange. "Here, help me rearrange the furniture. I have a sleeping bag I keep rolled up and stashed behind my couch."

Andrew and I looked at each other and smiled. Already we had private jokes. How had this happened so fast?

And what *was* this, anyway?

The desire to be desired by one you desire. My mind spun back to that old Jesuit priest in the cold stone chapel.

And so we stayed for the night—on the condition that I be allowed to cook dinner. I sent Coco and Webb to the neighborhood grocer's with a list. While they were gone, Andrew and I had a chance to fill Solange in on everything. She was still clapping her hands when the kids returned with food and flowers for everyone.

I made an old-fashioned, 100 percent predigital tuna casserole that I updated with a little Camembert, which Webb cutely removed and set to one side of his plate without comment. After dinner, Coco taught Webb how to make crème brûlée. They made a mess, but it was perfect.

On reflection, that's not a bad description for the whole trip. The kids made a mess, but it really *was* perfect. Because I realized that night I had exactly what I wanted and needed: a wonderful, quirky daughter who I didn't always understand and who clearly didn't always obey me. But she would do just fine in college—and, more important, in life.

I had a generous best friend who'd known me for twenty years and understood me better than I understood myself.

And I had a new friend: a kind man with a good heart and an adorable son.

There we were, the five of us, *cinco por cinco,* talking and laughing all night long. Nobody wrote an e-mail or sent a text. Nobody felt the need to get online. There was no steak sauce in sight. Or televisions—flat screen or otherwise.

Sometime after midnight Solange pushed Andrew out the door, purportedly because she wanted more wine. But it was clear she wanted to talk to me privately in the living room while Coco and Webb sang "MacArthur Park" and washed the dishes.

"He is an exhibit space designer," Solange reminded me in a whisper. "So you must give him space. Can you do that?"

"Of course," I whispered back, a bit defensively. "But Solange, don't rush me. Andrew and I just met a few days ago. And anyway, *I* need space, too."

"I know you do," she said. "But you have had a lifetime of space."

Solange looked at me hard. This was the woman who had known me when I was pregnant with Coco. She helped me make the hardest and best decision of my life. I was certain she was going to tell me, once again, to stop smoking, stop drinking, and stop feeling sorry for myself.

Solange's phone was ringing. "Damn that thing!" she said. She grabbed the phone and tossed it in the kitchen. "Coco, you can get this for me? Take a message."

"Sure thing," Coco said.

Solange refocused her attention on me. I could almost hear what she was going to say.

"I stopped smoking twenty years ago," I said, closing my eyes. "And I never have more than two glasses of wine."

"Uh-huh," Solange said sarcastically, holding an empty bottle in each hand.

"Okay, *almost* never," I admitted. "I really don't. If I do, I wake up with a crashing headache the next morning. As for feeling sorry for myself, I haven't and I don't, but even if I did—"

"Hey, Mom," Coco yelled from the kitchen.

"Just a second, honey," I answered.

"But *Mo-om,*" Coco continued.

That's when Solange put the wine bottles on the table and took my face in her hands.

"Dammit, Daisy," she said. "I can hear you through the wine. Stop talking and start feeling happy for yourself—"

"Mom," Coco interrupted. She was holding a dish towel in one hand and the phone in the other. "It's for you. It's Andrew."

I kissed Solange. Then I took the phone from my beautiful, capable daughter. I put the phone to my ear and said calmly and with confidence, "Hello."

Acknowledgments

I am grateful to many wonderful people who shared their time and talents with me as I wrote this book. Thanks to Kelly Bates-Siegel and Abby Adams for cheering me along from the very first draft. I am also hopelessly devoted to James Klise and Tim Bryant, both of whom I turned to often to ask, "What would a guy like Andrew be thinking now?" Even when I ignored your responses, I appreciated them. A big, name-in-lights thank-you to Elise Howard for introducing me to my brilliant editor, Lucia Macro. Thanks to Diahann Sturge for her page design wizardry. Of course I am grateful to Jimmy Webb for writing "Wichita Lineman," which is simply the best song in the whole wide world. And to the guy who slipped the note in my carry-on bag on that long-ago flight from St. Louis to Atlanta: whoever you are, wherever you are, thank you for planting the seed for this book.

Dawn Shields

Kate Klise

KATE KLISE spent fifteen years working as a correspondent for *People* magazine, covering everything from country music to reality TV to rappers, rockers, serial killers, and serial Sexiest Man Alive, Brad Pitt.

When she wasn't reporting for the magazine, Kate was home on her forty-acre Missouri farm, writing award-winning children's books such as *Regarding the Fountain*, *Dying to Meet You*, and *Grounded*.

In the Bag is Kate's first novel for adults—and the only book that was inspired by a handwritten note she found in her carry-on bag after a long flight.

For more about Kate Klise, vis www.kateklise.com.